The Choice

James Alexander

J&A PUBLISHING

Contents

CHAPTER ONE

The Choice

THE GROUP OF MEN circled Jared. His heart raced. They all carried guns and were bigger than him; each had already aced their initiations by murdering at least one person. He could feel their eyes on him, watching, as an old man cowered on the ground, pleading for his life.

A gang member close to him – he had not yet learned everyone's name – smiled and spat on the ground, nodding to Jared to do what needed to be done.

If only I could be at my old home, enjoying the sun in the backyard.

"How old are you kid?" the lead gang member asked.

Jared sized up the gang leader. Muscular and mean, he reminded him of a Rottweiler, bred for dogfighting.

Jared cleared his throat, "Fifteen."

"I can't hear you. You talk like a baby girl. What did you say?"

The man walked to stand in front of Jared and grabbed Jared's hair, yanking his head back. He heard a click in his neck at the force.

"I'm going to ask you again, and you are going to say in a loud voice, one like when some young chick is grabbing your balls and squeezing. You are going to say how old you are, so we can all hear you. We don't take sissies into our gang, especially a blond baby who can't talk like a man."

He let go of his hair and stepped back. "Now how old are you?"

Jared yelled this time, "Fifteen!"

The man nodded. "Good. Now prove to us you're a man!" the gangleader placed cold metal in his hands. A man in a dark trench coat and a hat stood behind the young men in the shadows. Jared couldn't get a good look at him, but he appeared to be older. Rain dripped off the man's hat, hiding his face.

He looked down to see it was a .38 caliber. His knees weakened. *I can't kill him! God, what do I do?* The old man cowered in front of him. He appeared homeless, pulled out of his makeshift hovel. But if I don't, I'm dead instead of him. Glancing up, his eyes darted around the circle of young men standing and waiting for him to pull the trigger. Images of him blowing the poor man's brains out made him queasy. The alley was empty, save for the young men, the stranger, and the scared old vagrant. The wind whipped through the street and the collar of his windbreaker snapped against his neck. He shivered from the breeze rushing through his clothes. The cool night air seemed to become dense and heavy with the violence about to ensue. He wondered if it was the grim reaper riding in to snatch its next victim's soul - his or the old man's.

The old man balanced on his knees, raising his hands up to Jared, pleading for him not to proceed with the task given to him. His face was full of whiskers and he reeked of booze.

A dark spot grew on the front of his pants. "Pleash, I dun nothin'," he cried out. "I, I have a boy, 'bout yur age." Tears streamed down his face.

"Just pop' him!" a large boy yelled.

"Slice is here to see you join us. Don't piss him off," the leader shouted.

Lightning struck in the distance and the sky filled with light. *Well, isn't that fitting? Nothing like making the situation more intense*, he thought as he looked down at the gun resting in his hands. Light reflected off the black barrel as another bolt of lightning graced the sky. He glanced back at the stranger in the background as the lightning flashed in the alley. The man's face appeared wrinkled and aged. A deep slice ran down the side of his face. *So that must be Slice.* He could see Slice as his lips curled into a sly smile. It chilled Jared to see him smile. It was as if a snake had seen its prey.

"Do it! Now!" another voice called out. He could sense the impatience in the man's loud voice.

The old man, though smelly and drunk, reminded him of his grandfather. He had spent countless summers with him and loved him dearly. It was last summer that he died of a heart attack. *God, I can't do this*, he thought. *I have to, or I am done.* He gritted his teeth with determination and slowly raised the gun to point it at the old man's head. *Just pull the trigger and be done with it*, he told himself. A siren in the near distance blared. The wind was whipping, throwing trash around in the air.

"God Dammit! Kill him now!" the leader shouted.

The gun shook as he held it – the barrel pointed at the old man. *Pull it you fool!* A blinding flash of light hit a trashcan not far up the alley and he could see his reflection in the glass from a nearby window. There he stood, about to make a decision that would shape his future. Rain dripped off his hair to his shoulders as if the sky was crying for him. Neither decision would have a good ending. The light faded and another bolt of lightning streaked the sky, followed by a deafening clap of thunder. *I'd never be able to live with myself.* Knowing what was to follow, he dropped the gun. He breathed a sigh of relief. It was the right thing to do. Another bolt of lightning followed. It was as though he were in the middle of a battle in the sky.

"No. I won't kill him." He focused on the ringleader, the largest of the crew closing in on him, cracking his knuckles, grinning. This would not be good. The old man looked up to him, his eyes narrowed, and Jared watched as he gave an understanding nod as if apologizing for the situation. He crawled backwards and through an open hole in the group of boys moving in to punish Jared.

The old man didn't make it far. Jared could see him as he bumped into Slice. One moment, the vagrant thought he was free, the next he had a gaping wound in his stomach spewing blood and a dark fluid to the wet pavement. Slice raised his head to focus on Jared, the knife still dripping blood. The old man held his middle and was moaning. It sounded as though a stray cat was giving birth, deep and guttural.

The leader stepped forward. "I offer you protection, and you do this? You refuse me, you refuse us. Over a drunk?" he motioned to the old man in a pool of blood. "You're dead, like him." Slice gripped the old man's head and sliced his throat open. Jared felt his knees buckle at the sight.

Pain spread through Jared's back. He wondered if he heard the padded "thunk" sound first or felt the pain first. He fell to his knees and saw what appeared to be a bat in one of the thug's hands. He tried to block another attack aimed at his face with a nightstick. It hit his forearm and it popped as the nightstick hit bone, followed by a crunch as it broke through his cheekbone. Red filled his vision and his face was wet. He wished it were just the rain, but knew differently. Falling face-first into the tar, he curled into a fetal position. Pain spread over his body as he took countless hits from many attackers. *All for a homeless drunk*, he thought. Pain stabbed him from everywhere on his body.

Another flash brightened the sky as he stared up past the faces grinning at the hurt they were causing. A bright bolt darted past clouds, branching out in several directions. He saw Slice looking down on him, that sly smile on his wrinkled and worn face again.

Slice pulled Jared's head back, pulling his hair to expose his neck. *He's going to kill me.* His vision faded and his eyes stung from blood dripping down his forehead. A familiar noise rang in his ears and he tried to focus on it. *Police!*

Jared expected cold steel running across his windpipe; instead the old man leaned close to his ear. He could feel the man breathing. "Nobody denies Slice. I won't end this here. If you live, I'll get you and I'll make you suffer. I'll slice you and slice you. I'll make you last. You will wish for the death that bum received." Slice pushed his head to the wet tar.

"Time to go! We can finish this later," the leader yelled.

"Man, look at him! The punk's bleedin' out!" another voice shouted, followed by laughter and then the sound of footsteps running away.

A moment passed and more footsteps approached.

"Son, hang in there. I need an ambulanc-, " the voice cut out and blackness closed around him.

***

Thunder boomed above, and to Jared's surprise, he stood looking down at the .38. Instead of dropping the gun, he brought it up to aim at the old man's head and pulled the trigger. He wanted to stop himself, but couldn't. Someone else or some force had the control. The emotions frightened him. It wasn't remorse or shock, but exhilaration. He had the power over this person. He chose whether he lived or died. Of course, the right thing to do was to kill him. That's what a real man would do. The strong live, the weak die - easy as that. He smiled at the thought. Blood spattered the tar and the man's body fell backwards into a lifeless heap. The body twitched and red covered the ground. Red contrasting with the blackness of the night was quite beautiful. The gang came forward and patted him on the back for a job well done. Slice stood behind the men, clapping. A moment later, he turned and vanished down the alley. *They respect me!* A blinding flash stung his eyes.

***

"Clear!"

Flash! Darkness.

"Clear!"

Flash! Beep, Beep, Beep.

"I don't believe it. We've got a pulse." A voice echoed through a fog.

Pain spread through him, but was soon vanquished by a needle in his veins. Deep sleep followed.

CHAPTER TWO

Prison

OPEN YOUR EYES! JARED yelled at himself and tried as hard as he could to do it, but it was no use. Voices came to him from the distance, muffled as if blocked by pillows. He searched out their source and quickly grew tired. This had become a usual event. He'd try time and time again, but would always grow tired and the blackness would surround him.

Warmth spread through him when he noticed someone, who he imagined to be his mother, touch his hand. He couldn't understand how he knew it was his mother sitting near him, he just did. *How long has it been? What is happening? Mom! Are you there? Please!* He tried to yell out, but it was no good.

"I can't take this anymore!" his mother said.

"Please Lana, have faith. He's a strong boy," his father replied wearily.

"It's been three years, John," her voice wavered, "I can't take seeing him like this. The doctors keep saying he's never going to come back."

Three years! God. Why can't I open my eyes? He tried to thrash out. Nothing. He tried harder. Nothing. *Please, Mom! I'm here!* It was no use. No one heard him except for himself.

"Lana! You can't talk like that. He needs us," his dad replied in a controlled tone.

"John, you must let go. What would you want me to do if it were you? I love him, John, and it tears me apart to have to think like this, but he is already gone, sweetheart."

No, I'm not! Mom, I'm not. I'm here. Jared wanted to cry. He tried to move something, anything. Nothing.

"Lana, I'd never forgive myself. Ever."

"I know, honey. I know." She was crying. Jared's father joined her.

"It's not fair. Why did it have to happen to him? It's my fault," John paused a moment and took a deep breath before continuing, "I never should have pushed us to move."

"No. It's not your fault. We did what we had to do, just like we will do what we have to do now. We are his parents, John, and we need to help our son when he needs help. He needs to move on."

"Tomorrow," he replied.

Shit! I can get out of this. Please. I don't want to die yet! he thought. This had been the longest period yet of being aware of things around him. *If only I didn't go out that night.* It was only supposed to be a friend showing him around the city and maybe going to see a movie. His friend told him he belonged to a gang, but he never imagined he'd try to bring him in on it as well. *If I get out of here, I'm going to pay him a visit,* he thought. It then occurred to him that his friend might be dead by now.

"It's always tomorrow, John. We need to do this now. We're barely hanging on as it is - I," her voice shook, she paused to steady her voice, "I just can't take seeing our baby like this anymore."

"Tomorrow, I promise."

Warm air brushed his cheek as his mom leaned over to kiss him goodbye, followed by sounds of footsteps fading away. He wanted to drift off to the blackness again, but fought the pull of the abyss. *No! I need to fight this or tomorrow I'm dead.*

More footsteps approached. A woman's voice, a beautiful voice, began singing a song he did not know. Gentle hands slid under him and rolled him to his side. The sound of water dripped into a bucket as if a sponge were being wrung out. She ran the sponge down his back. *Weak prick, I can't even wash myself. God knows how many times some pretty girl changed my messed sheets*, he chided himself and wanted to cry again.

"I know you're there, Jared, and I know you can beat this," her voice told him.

Please tell me how! Please! He tried to yell, but again, no sound escaped his lips.

"Time is running out, Jared, you need to pull through this."

Another voice, this time deeper, interrupted her.

"You done with the scrub-down yet, Kate? Don't spend too much time on this one. He's on his way out. Machines are going to be shut down tomorrow. Already spoke with the parents." His voice seemed unusually upbeat.

"Frank, do you really need to talk that way in front of a patient, comatose or not?"

"Oh, get over yourself, honey. It happens to them all."

The woman rolled him over to his back again and placed her hand on his chest. He smelled a flowery scent. It was so good to sense something long lost to him. Her voice whispered in his ear.

"Don't listen to him."

She walked out and Jared heard a slap followed by a yelp from the woman. "Try that again and I'll report you for sexual harassment."

She kept walking and the door closed behind her. The darkness called to him, its peacefulness beckoning for him to drift off and to forget about his problems, leaving the emotional pain behind. Instead, he lay there, focusing on every muscle in his body, searching for the one that might give in and set him free.

The hours passed and he became exhausted. From time to time, his mind would drift and he would see himself. In the vision he was not confined to a hospital bed, but roaming the streets, a gang of followers behind him. Sometimes, he was selling bags filled with white powder to kids; other times he'd be roughing up some poor person. Age didn't matter. Whoever looked at him the wrong way caused intense anger and he'd lash out, his crew following his lead. He saw himself in drive-by shootings, taking down enemy gang members, often hitting innocent people in the crossfire. He'd feel a pang of guilt from time to time, but would push it aside.

Memories of his own life would rush back to him. *I am in a bed. This is not me. Thank God, this is not me! I would never hurt anyone like that...not me!* he would tell himself and his focus would return to trying to move.

A new sensation overwhelmed him. Had he moved his finger? Something was different. Countless times, he had tried to move something – anything – and this time he had. He tried again, but the communication of having twitched some small muscle in his finger did not reoccur. The knowledge of time had long disappeared from him. He figured he must have spent hours trying to replicate the movement and shamed himself for not being able to. Exhausted from his exertion, he faded out, unable to withstand the pull of the darkness he so desperately wanted to avoid.

CHAPTER THREE

Comatose Dreamz

"Son, I'm so sorry. I should have been there for you. I hope you'll find peace and happiness. Please forgive me." His voice was unsteady. He cleared his throat.

"John, it's not your fault. You know that," Jared's mother said, comforting his father.

"Are you sure you want to do this? There might still be a chance. He fought hard to survive this long." This voice sounded like the woman who had washed his back the previous night. Jared tried to remember her name. *Cathy?* The name didn't fit. He concentrated harder. *Kate! Her name is Kate!*

"This is not your concern. Do you have any idea how hard this is for my wife and me? This isn't a decision we are making without any thought," his father said, using a carefully controlled tone.

Move. Move, you idiot! You're going to die! Jared thought and tried moving the finger he had felt twitch the night before. Nothing.

"Kate, please go and help the patient next door," a deep voice that Jared knew to be the doctor's said and then paused. "Mr. and Mrs. Stone had to make a hard decision and we need to respect that."

The sound of the doctor's voice stirred something in Jared. Heat radiated in his skin. It was anger. It felt good to feel angry again. At least he was feeling something—even if it was negative. He recalled the doctor's name from the previous day when he had picked on the poor nurse. *Frank*. Jared felt a surge of pride and if he'd been able to smile, he would have. Pieces were starting to come together and stay together. No longer were they fragmented memories that made no sense.

"I'm really sorry, that's not what I was implying. Doctor, it's only that he is still retaining the fluids well, and he appears to be healthy," Kate said.

"Enough! Kate, please leave," the doctor replied.

Ok, finger, move. Please! Jared focused as hard as he could. There! He sensed motion in his index finger.

He heard someone leave the room. Frank's voice echoed through again.

"I'm sorry about Kate. She is very emotional. She means well, but sometimes she oversteps."

Jared clawed in the darkness, trying to find his way back to the state of consciousness he had been in before slipping off the night before. His father's voice echoed through the darkness.

"No, we understand," his mom replied. "This isn't easy for us. Are you sure he won't have pain?"

Why? Look at me. I can move. I can move! Jared moved his finger once more, but no one was watching.

"I assure you, Mrs. Stone, he won't feel anything. We are only providing food and nutrients to keep him alive. Once we shut that down, he will pass peacefully in a few days," the doctor paused while his father blew his nose. "Remember, he is not conscious, so he will not feel any different."

"Please do it then," she said in a resolute tone.

A hand wrapped around his arm and he felt something being withdrawn. *No! I'm here. Why aren't you looking? I'm here! Mom! Dad!* Jared searched for another way to get their attention, but he was unable to move anything else. He tried to move his finger again, but it was no use. He heard his parents stand up and his mom kissed him on the cheek.

"I love you, Jared." She began to cry and left the room.

His father squeezed his arm. "I love you, son."

Frank was still in the room, opening and closing drawers. His footsteps approached the bed. Jared sensed the doctor staring down at him as he sat down in the chair next to Jared's bed. *One more time.* Jared focused on his hand and twitched his finger again.

"I know you're there, kid. You don't need to prove anything to me. I've seen lots of people like you come in and waste away, twitching fingers, toes, eyelashes. The point is, you're a drain on the system. All that money wasted on vegetables like you when others could lead lives. Yet they don't receive the care because of you idiots draining the system. No, your time is up." Frank laughed and left the room, closing the door behind him.

What now? What can I do? The abyss beckoned, and he drifted off into the blackness—or at least what should have been blackness.

***

He found himself walking down a dark street. Three other men were behind him. In his hand he held a black pistol and his fingers ran over some engraving on the hilt of the gun. He looked down to see "J-Rock" spelled out in gold lettering.

"Yo! What'up, J?" a man asked from behind him.

Confused, he turned around to see three men staring at him. The most muscular of the three spat, his arms crossed. He adjusted his hood to cover more of his face, his gold chain clanking as it moved. Jared could make out a gold front tooth.

"Where am I? Who are you? And why do I have a gun in my hand? Better yet, how the hell am I walking?" Jared asked.

The men around him started laughing. The man next to "Gold Tooth", who was much smaller and had a nasty gash on his cheek, joined in. "Look like J got in da stash!" He spat on the ground and Jared couldn't help but stare at the nasty wound on the man's cheek. *I'll call him "Gash" because that's all I can see when I look at him. Damn, that is nasty,* Jared thought as he watched Gash laugh. "He worse den you, Fatty!" Gash wheeled around and hit the third man on his shoulder.

It was no wonder why they gave Fatty his name. He appeared to be at least three hundred pounds. Even with the fat, he looked as though he could lift a Mac truck clear off the ground. Fatty frowned at Gash and the other man backed off in a hurry.

"Just messin wid ya." Gash tried to calm the bigger man down before he turned him into a pancake.

Gold Tooth stepped closer to Jared, his head lowered. Jared's pulse quickened and he spotted the man's thumb twitching where he held his pistol. *I'm in a gang. This isn't good. If I look weak, they'll kill me.* Jared glanced at the two other men behind Gold Tooth. They both stood watching.

"If you are high man, I'll kill you myself. I aint following a junkie to war." Gold Tooth sneered at him as he spoke.

Stay cool. He raised the gun to point it at the other man. "Don't mess with me. I should kill you for questioning me." He nodded to the two men behind Gold Tooth, "Yo, you both wid me? Or this clown?" he motioned the gun at Gold Tooth. "I'll make sure you both are rewarded. Choose wisely."

The two men drew their own guns and pointed them at Gold Tooth, who was now backing down, his hand shaking slightly on his own gun, pointed at the ground.

"Nah man, it all cool. I wid you, J." Gold Tooth's voice shook as he spoke.

Going to piss himself, Jared relished the thought, but he didn't know why. It felt good to push fear into someone. *This isn't me! Why do I feel this way?* He lowered his gun.

A noise erupted from behind where Jared stood. He saw Gash jump back at the sound. Jared wheeled around to see five other men, all wearing green bandannas around their heads. Each of them were carrying guns, one of which was pointed at him. A loud pop sounded as a burst of smoke erupted from its barrel. A sickening, crushing noise rang in his mind and pain spread from his shoulder as he fell backward to the ground.

FLASH!

***

The pain had disappeared and the familiar blackness covered him like a cozy blanket. *What is happening to me? Am I dying already?* Jared embraced the darkness.

CHAPTER FOUR

Sequins and Feathers

THE REHAB CENTER WAS eerily quiet. Most of the daytime staff had left for the evening. It felt good to be out of the standard garb that management required medical staff to wear. Dr. Frank Ryan checked to make sure he had his keys in his pocket as he made his way to the exit; passing by the nurses' station, he saw Kate reviewing a document. He walked up from behind her, stopping short of bumping into her. She didn't turn to see who was standing behind her.

"Doctor, you need to back off. I'm not kidding. I will report your behavior." Kate shook her head and turned to face him, her cheeks reddened. "We need to talk about what happened today. I don't like the way you treated me in front of those people."

Frank didn't move. He smiled at her. "I've been here a long time, little lady, and I've seen young nurses like you come and go. If you think anyone is going to do anything about your petty complaints, you need to think again." He winked at her through his smudgy glasses and continued. "Now that we've got that little bit of *nothingness* out of the way, how about we go to dinner? I can't wait to see what's under those scrubs."

Kate threw her hands up in the air and groaned before storming down the hall.

"Little pussycat is upset?" he hollered to her as she walked away. *I hate having to act this way. I can't take it anymore!* he thought to himself and softly shook his head.

Rolling up his plaid shirtsleeve, he looked down at his wrist to the Rolex hidden underneath. It was getting late, and he wanted to be home.

Traffic wasn't too bad and he liked the ride between work and home. It gave him a few moments to adjust from his 'work mode' to his 'home mode.' Plus, he loved driving his new Toyota Prius. He rolled the window down and breathed in the evening air as he drove to a stop at an intersection and checked his hair in the rearview mirror. A stray hair dangled over his forehead. Wrinkling his nose, he grabbed the comb sitting in the storage compartment and brushed his hair back into place. *God, I hate flyaways!* He cringed at the thought that the public has seen him with such messy hair.

A man in skinny jeans and a tight V-neck T-shirt was walking his dog on the sidewalk. Frank saw him and turned to watch him walk by; he jumped when the car behind him honked to tell him to move on. Frank could see the man smiling at him as he began to drive again. Frank laughed to himself. *How embarrassing! My goodness, Frank!* he thought as he turned on the radio. Heavy metal blared from the station selection from this morning. Sometimes he would carpool with his coworker Dana, a doctor as well. Dana liked the heavy metal music and Frank didn't want to seem weak, so he lied to him and said that he liked it too. Now he was stuck listening to it every morning, in the event it was a carpool day. He immediately switched it to classical and continued his drive home.

A few minutes passed and Frank was pulling into his driveway. He parked the car under the carport and stretched when he stood up. *Finally!* he sighed and proceeded to unlock the door to his home. Princess, his Chihuahua, was yapping at the noise he was causing. She jumped on his leg when he opened the door to the kitchen, realizing it was her owner and not an intruder. The trapped air in the room was stale, so he opened a window to let in a fresh breeze. Frank paused and stared at the red message light on the phone signaling a missed call. "I bet it's Dad!" he sighed, and knelt down to pick up the dog.

"How's my pretty little lady?" He brought the dog's nose to his lips and gave her a few kisses. Princess returned the smooches by licking his face.

Ignoring the message light, he set the dog down and walked to the sitting room. This was his favorite time of day; the time of day he could do what he wanted to do. Reaching into his pocket, he withdrew another key. This key unlocked the door to his other life, the life he kept hidden from everyone. Smiling, he unlocked the door and swung it open. A group of mannequin stood in front of him. The middle one donned his latest creation, a vest with layers upon layers of bright feathers. Spandex shorts adorned with sparkly sequins hugged the mannequin's hips.

"Oh Princess, I'm so happy with our creation, aren't you?" He looked down at the dog as it tried to get its master's attention with yaps between licks.

He walked over to where the mannequins stood and knelt down to pick up the matching outfit for Princess - a blanket with two little holes for her front legs. Princess's outfit was also covered in feathers.

Small purple undies with three holes, two for her back legs and one for her tail, lay under the blanket.

Princess ran over to him, hoping for some affection, but Frank, instead of petting her, dressed her in her new outfit. She looked up at him, her eyes wide, not quite sure what to make of her attire and tried her best to shake it off, but it was no use. Frank had expected that she'd try to break free of it, so he included straps with Velcro to keep it all in place. Setting her down, she took off to a corner and tried her best to break free of his fashion breakthrough. Frank changed into his spandex shorts, smiling at the sight of the fabric hugging his hips.

"What do you think, Princess? I love the sparkle, don't you?" he arched his back and stuck his butt out at the dog before giggling. "If only Daddy knew what his son was up to!" His smile faded at the thought and he frowned. Princess yapped at him and he smiled at her. "I know. I don't know why I let him get to me." He shrugged and put on the vest, buttoning it tight.

"Now, for the grand finale!" He walked over to the closet and opened the door. A fluffy boa hung from a hook in the middle of the door; he grabbed it and threw over his shoulder. "Done!" He clapped as he spoke and ran over to where Princess was still fidgeting with her outfit. Ignoring the licks of affection, Frank picked her up and carried her to stand with him in front of the full length mirror in the room.

"Oh Princess! You are so cute! Don't you love it?" He scratched the dog's chin and she licked his hand in return.

Turning to look at the back of his outfit in the mirror, he slapped his butt with his free hand and scowled. "My, my! Getting a little junk in the trunk!" He pursed his lips. "Well, no one's perfect, are they, Princess?"

The phone rang in the other room and Frank scowled, letting Princess down before rushing to the phone. *I bet it's that bastard father of mine!* he thought before picking up the receiver and resting it against his ear.

"Son?" It was his father's voice.

Frank cleared his throat and tried his deeper voice, "Hi, Jim," he replied.

"I've been trying to reach you for days. Where have you been?"

"Work, sir."

"That's my boy. Chasing the mighty dollar. I hope chasing some pretty tail too." He laughed. "Pushing you into a medical career was the best thing I ever did for you. I'm sure you realize that now, don't you, Frank?"

"Yes, sir, I do."

Jim laughed. "You remember when you got that dumb-ass idea in your head about going into fashion or whatever the hell it was? I hope to God you're not doing any stupid shit like that again."

"No, sir," Frank adjusted his spandex. One of the stitches from the sequins he had sewn on the fabric was scratching against his skin. *I'll have to fix that*, he thought to himself.

"That's my boy. You know, Son, I'm proud of you. I was a bit worried about how you were turning out when you were in school." The silence lasted a moment. "Well, you know, when you were wearing that-" he cleared his throat, "well, it doesn't matter. You turned out just fi ne."

"Sir, why did you call me? To harass me?" Frank shifted his weight and glanced at the clock.

"No, Son, I called because I'm not feeling my best. I'm going to die soon and that's that. I won't drag this out more than I have to. You're my only heir."

"OK, great, Dad. Listen, I have to go." Not waiting for his reply, Frank hung up the phone and ran his hands through his hair. "Asshole!"

Frank paced the room, Princess following behind, hoping for some random scrap of food to fall even though Frank had none to give. He ran his hands through his hair again and took a deep breath as a tear streamed down his cheek. Coming to a stop, he leaned against the counter and slipped down to the floor. The tight spandex stretched, resisting as best it could from tearing. Princess ran to sit on his lap and Frank patted the dog's head. Frank leaned his head back against the cabinet. Memories of his childhood rushed through his mind. It had not been a happy existence; all he ever wanted was his father's acceptance.

"He'll never understand, will he, Princess?" Frank smiled as his little dog looked at him, her eyes pleading for his affection. "But you do, don't you?" Leaning forward, he kissed the dog's mouth and let her lick his lips.

Frank took another deep breath and wiped away his tears. "Be strong, Frank. Someday . . ." his voice trailed off as he looked at a picture of his father, dressed in his military suit. "Someday soon, he'll experience the pain he has given me, my whole life."

The clock sounded that the hour had changed. Frank jumped and looked at the time. "Oh, my! Already?" He gave Princess one more pat on the head and ran into the entertainment room to turn on the TV.

The newest fashion reality show was on. Princess was at his heels. He picked her up and ran to the couch to sit down. Covered in feathers and sequins, he watched with envy. Envious of those who were fulfilling their dreams. Those that did not care what their over-demanding fathers and mothers thought.

Chapter Five

Death in a Needle

Unable able to cope with his situation any longer, Jared was finding it more and more difficult to focus on trying to move. His need for food and water was making him weaker and more tired with each passing day. His stomach grumbled; it felt as though it was closing in on itself. The pain was tremendous, but the thirst was even worse. His parents would stop by each day to kiss and hug him, but no one ever noticed any of the slight movements he was able to make. The only person who had seen anything had been the creepy doctor, and he wasn't about to do anything. *Bastard!* Jared thought to himself, vowing to teach the jerk a lesson if he ever made it out of his comatose state.

The sound of approaching footsteps alerted him to what was going on around him. Someone was sitting near him and he realized that it was Kate. She always wore a flowery perfume that he loved. She would often sit by him and flip through pages as if she were reading a magazine. He had come to love the time that she would spend in his room, even if she didn't talk. It was nice to know that someone was nearby. His stomach rumbled. He needed food. *I'm so hungry! I need to get out of this. Please Kate, help me!*

"Kate? What are you doing? He's a waste of your time." Jared recognized the doctor's voice.

"He's a patient, Doctor. He deserves attention just like everyone else." Her tone was sharp.

"He's wasting away. I'm watching over him. Go coddle someone else."

"One of these days, the way you talk around patients will catch up to you." The sound of the chair scraping the floor meant she must have stood up. "He might still come around, you never know."

Frank laughed. "What? You can't be serious! I've been a doctor here a long time, Kate. I know when someone will come around and when they won't. Why don't you go play with some dolls, little girl, and let me deal with the big boy world?"

Jared focused on trying to move his finger while he knew Kate was nearby. *Come on Kate! Please notice!* He pushed himself.

"How dar—" she stopped mid-sentence. "Frank! Frank! He moved his finger!"

"No. That's not possible." Frank stepped closer and Jared moved it again.

"See, he did!" Kate's voice filled with excitement.

"No, I've seen things like this before, Kate. It's a reflex as his body dies. That's all."

Jared found he was able to squeeze one of his eyelids. *How's that, dick-wad?* he laughed to himself. *Reflex? Finally, someone sees. I'm so damned hungry.*

"Kate, I need to check this out further. Can you please go get me my glasses?"

"I'd rather hook his IV back up if you don't mind."

"Kate! Go get my glasses. Don't make me ask again. We need to be sure it's not a simple reflex before we contact his family or make any change to what they had requested. Please, Kate. My glasses."

"He's healing, Frank. I know he is. I'll go get your glasses." Jared heard her leave the room, but before doing so, he heard a strange click. It amazed Jared how strong his hearing had become. It was his only conduit to the world outside of the perpetual blackness that trapped him. A moment passed and Frank leaned in close.

"You little bastard. You're going to die either by natural means or with a bit of help." Frank uncapped something. "Did I ever tell you that I never wanted to be a doctor? I hate my damned job. Dealing with useless bags of waste like you, it makes me sick." Jared caught a whiff of the doctor's breath. The doctor must have been leaning right over him. His breath reeked of garlic. It was disgusting, but at the same time, it made Jared's stomach grumble again. It had been so long since he'd had any solid food.

The doctor continued, "So I kill all you shits whenever I can, and one day I will get caught." He laughed a little. "But I don't care. I can finally bring my stupid father down a few pegs and he'll realize what a horrible job he did raising me. He'll die a bitter old man." Frank grabbed Jared's arm. "Here in this little needle is your ticket out of this world. The cops will come in and as usual won't spot the little prick in your arm. They never do." Frank squeezed his arm looking for a good vein. "So that's our little secret. You can tell everyone that you see wherever you go after this stupid life."

Jared's mind raced. *Why? Please. Don't do this!*

"Frank?" Kate asked. Her voice shook.

Frank released his grip on Jared's arm and let the needle drop, kicking it under the bed. "Oh, I was checking his pulse, where are my glasses?"

"I saw the needle, Frank. What were you giving him? He's not supposed to have any medication."

"No, I don't have a needle."

"Frank, I saw you drop it. It's under the bed."

"How dare you question me?" Frank yelled at her.

"I heard your conversation through the intercom. I switched it on before I left. I didn't trust you; now I know why." She shook her head. "I called the police."

"You little bi—!" Frank yelled as pushed himself away from where Jared lay helpless.

Kate, run! Jared thought. Kate had become his only hope. Everyone else had turned their backs on him. They'd given up on him. Except Kate. He was so close to beating this thing. Just a little more time. Now, Frank would hurt her and there was nothing he could do about it.

Jared heard her footsteps rush away. The sound of a scream pierced his ears.

"Let go of me!" Kate shouted.

"I can't now," Frank grunted. "I'm sorry, Kate. I didn't want this to happen."

SMACK!

Jared's pulse raced. *I'm useless. A useless slug.*

Frank cried out, "You hit me, you bitch!"

A loud crash of something or *someone* flailing against a wall followed. Kate gasped for air. More footsteps approached.

A woman's voice, one Jared did not recognize, asked, "What is going on here?" her voice unsteady. "Kate, dear, are you OK?"

"Get Out! Everyone out! I've got a knife and I'll kill anyone who gets close to me!" Frank yelled.

"Frank, the police are coming. Stop now," Kate pleaded.

"Get out, Kate, or I'll kill your patient and anyone else that gets in my way."

The door slammed, followed by a click. Frank dragged something heavy and slammed it against what Jared imagined to be the door. They were locked in the room together.

He's going to kill me. This is it! Jared's stomach turned. He wasn't hungry now. The rumblings of hunger had long since disappeared.

Frank ran to the bed and grabbed Jared by his shoulders, shaking. "My life is ruined because of you and that stupid nurse! I knew I would get caught someday, but I'm not ready yet!"

Jared heard him slide down to the floor and the doctor began to cry.

"My life has been such a waste. I should have been great — a brilliant designer, like I dreamed of. Instead, I did everything my bastard father wanted." Frank gasped for air as he sobbed. "Princess. Who is going to take care of Princess?"

Princess? Jared figured the doctor wasn't right in the head, but who the heck was Princess?

There were several knocks at the door, followed by a man's voice, "Open the door. It's the police!"

Frank still sat near Jared's bed, sobbing. "She's the only one that loves me." He sobbed some more.

Someone tried to push the door open. It sounded as though whatever was blocking the door had given slightly. "Open the door!"

Jared heard the doctor fish under the bed for the needle.

"If you do ever wake up, kid, tell my Dad I'll see him in Hell."

Frank cried a minute longer and took a deep breath. The sobbing stopped as did any movement from below where Jared lay.

CHAPTER SIX

Voices of the Almost Dead

"Hey Kane!" a piece of paper flew by Detective Kane's face and landed a few feet away from where he sat. "Surprised you didn't foresee that coming!" Detective Crange yelled at him and the other detectives laughed.

Crange was referring to Kane's last case, where he had a "hunch" by way of discussion with the deceased victim when reviewing a crime scene. The victim was a prominent citizen, an old man who had been tied to a bed and force-fed an entire bottle of Viagra. The suspect left him to die alone. A voice — the deceased's — had entered Kane's mind, accusing the old man's long-time mistress of the murder. The old man's spirit told Kane that his mistress was fed up with waiting for him to divorce his wife so they could finally live together. She later decided that if she couldn't have him, no one would. The deceased directed Kane to look in the cardboard compactor outside a nearby restaurant. Kane followed the voice's orders and, sure enough, found an empty bottle of Viagra hidden under collapsed rice boxes.

The prescription tag matched the name of the victim's. Besides the fingerprints of the victim, another unidentified set were on the bottle. With a little more research, he had found out who the mistress was and gathered enough evidence to bring her in for questioning. She of course broke down and confessed. Between her confession and the damning fingerprints from the bottle, Kane had closed the case.

Kane had always had strange visions and would often hear voices, but he would keep it to himself. With his luck, someone would commit him to the loony bin and he'd lose his job. In the end, he thought it best for no one else to know. Yet his visions always led him in the right direction and he grew tired of having to hide it all the time. He decided to change that after he closed the Viagra case.

When asked by a reporter how he had been able to close the case so quickly, he finally came clean and explained. The media, of course, had a field day with the insight into Kane's "abilities" and he became the laughingstock of the force. Luckily, he had such a good record at closing cases that the only consequence was a reprimand from his boss that he could no longer talk to the media in any way.

***

Kane looked back to his desk, ignoring the usual, constant verbal abuse he suffered from his peers. Stacks of paper containing information on unsolved cases stood in front of him and taunted him like everyone else. It didn't bother him though. He had become used to overwhelming volumes of work. *There's never any shortage of work in criminal justice,* he thought to himself as he looked down at a folder full of information on a gang member case he had been working on since he began his career as a detective five years ago. He had been tracking the gang for some time, trying to get to the ringleader, but it had been so well constructed, all leads resulted in dead ends and all witnesses murdered. Like a spider web, the gang had spiraled deep into the community and had far-reaching connections. If one was unlucky enough to have somehow offended a member of the gang, he or she would wind up dead on a doorstep shortly thereafter.

Kane sighed. *All these years and I cannot get anywhere with this guy.* The leader, known only as "Slice," was a shadow. No one knew his identity or anything about him other than that he was called Slice because of the scar on his face that he had gotten from one of his knife fights. He was always the victor and his adversary was always left for dead, the victim's abdomen a gaping hole from the repeated slicing he made into his signature move. As far as Kane knew there was only one person outside of his inner circle of gang members who had survived after seeing Slice, and it would have been easier for the victim if he had died. He was now comatose and had been since being beaten to within an inch of his life for refusing to participate in the gang initiation. Doctors had told Kane that the boy's chances of waking from his coma were close to nil.

Kane jumped when his radio sounded. He liked to stay informed of things going on should they relate to any of his cases. It was amazing how events and people were so intertwined with each other. The dispatcher reported a situation involving a patient at a local rehabilitation center, his life being threatened by one of the doctors. *Well, something like that doesn't happen every day*, he shook his head in amazement. It wasn't until he heard the name Jared Stone that he became interested in finding out more. *Jared Stone. Jared Stone. Where the hell have I heard that name?* He put his head down to rest in his hands. He was staring down at the folder of all the victims who had died from Slice's knife and he flipped through the documents before stopping at the picture of the young man lying helpless in a comatose state in a hospital bed. Underneath the photo was a note:

"Jared Stone, gang beaten. Coma. Slice may have been at the scene."

He took a deep breath and slammed the folder shut. *Holy Shit! Jared Stone. Maybe Slice was trying to finish the job?* He jumped to his feet, grabbed his jacket, and turned to leave when he remembered he didn't have his keys. "Shit!" he muttered, opened the drawer and fumbled around for the keys. He found them and turned to leave again. On his way out, he heard Crange whispering to another detective.

"Oh look! Wonder Boy saw someone else swallowing some Viagra." Crange laughed and the other detective laughed with him.

Kane ignored the comment and kept walking. *Laugh, you idiots. I will solve another case, while you sit on your asses and do nothing as usual.*

"Jared Stone," he muttered as he ran to his car, a beat-up station wagon from the 80s. Fake wood trim ran along the side of the car. Kane found that his car had become another source of repeated jokes. "Why would someone want to kill him? Maybe he's waking up?" His heart pounded as he spoke his thoughts out loud. Whenever he got excited, he'd start talking to himself, which of course did not help him defend himself against the insanity accusations. *Imagine if he is waking, then he might be able to help identify Slice.* He whistled as he imagined getting closer to finding the gang leader. The door to the old car groaned as he opened it. Crossing his fingers, he tried to start the car. It chugged for a minute before stalling out.

"Oh, come on! Not now!" He tried again and a puff of smoke shot out the back. Applying some more gas, the car kept running this time. Not wanting to waste any time, he pulled out the portable police light and stuck it to the roof of the car before pulling out with a squeal. Kane loved his car. It wasn't pretty to look at, but the V8 under the hood was a powerhouse many new cars lacked. Sure, it hurt at the gas pump, but it purred and he loved the deep, throaty noise it made as he applied the accelerator. A small picture of him, his wife, and daughter was in the corner of the rearview mirror; he glanced at and smiled.

Cars moved aside as he drove as fast as he could through the city. Not noticing a pothole, the car jerked, sending his coffee mug, half-filled with stale coffee, flying into the air to come to a rest in Kane's lap. "Dah! Stupid mug!" he shouted as he fumbled to lift it back upright, coffee spattering his pants and shirt. *I guess that's why they call it a travel mug — it travels. Waste of money.* He sighed and set the mug back in the holder. Kane had grown used to coffee stains. It seemed every morning, somehow, he always managed to spill coffee on himself. His wife would not be happy to see he had gotten another stain.

Approaching the patient facility, he could see that the police had already arrived and the ambulance was parked near the entrance. *I hope he's OK. He's my only lead!* He pulled the car to a stop near the other police cars and quickly got out, unlatching the strap keeping his gun in place near his hip. It had been a long time that he'd been after Slice.

***

It had become much more important that Slice be brought to justice after a failed attempt on his family's lives. As Kane took in the scene, memories of the night he had nearly lost his life protecting his family from a home invasion crept into his mind. Memories of the gunman holding his wife made his heart pound. It was close — too close. He could be a widower right now. That was when he vowed to bring down Slice; it was he who had sent the thugs to take out his family. Luckily, with the help of his partner at the time, Kane had taken down the man holding his wife. Shots were fired and Kane was able to take the other two men out, but his partner was killed. Amazingly, his family was unscathed — other than being shaken up — and his daughter, the joy of his life, was now happily living her toddler years. He smiled at the thought of her running wild through the house.

***

Medics carted a stretcher out; the outline of a body, covered by a sheet, worried him. He brought his attention back to the present. Kane ran over to the medics and showed his badge. The medics stopped and allowed him to move back the sheet covering the man's head. He breathed a sigh of relief at what he saw. *It's not Jared.* He looked up at the medics.

"What happened to the patient?" he asked.

One medic shrugged. "This one is the only one that we were told to take." They kept moving to avoid being seen by too many gawkers.

Everyone loves a show. Kane smoothed out his shirt, glancing down at the brown coffee stain covering the front and shook his head before walking into the building. The air reeked of the chemicals used to clean up the bodily fluids that all hospitals seemed to emanate mixed with the stale smell of bodies unused, either comatose patients or dying elderly. *Makes you realize how good you have it, even with coffee stains on your shirt,* he thought to himself as he walked to Jared's ward. He took a moment to remember which hallway to take as he had given up on the poor kid. Kane walked past a door and stopped when he heard a voice. He looked around, but no one was there. The voice kept talking and he focused on the sound.

"Please. Let me die," the voice said.

Again, he looked around, but no one was near. *Idiot! I really am losing it. The police psychologist would love to hear this!* He laughed, but the voice came through again.

I want to die. Please.

Kane rolled his eyes. "Shut up already!" he exclaimed in a quiet tone. He turned toward the voice. A closed door stood in front of him, but it had a small window in its center. Curiously, he peered inside. A body of an old man lay in a lone bed. The patient was connected to an IV and an electronic breathing device. His eyes were closed and he looked dead already. Rubbing his forehead, Kane moved on before stopping at another voice, this time a woman's: *Tom, I'm so sorry. It was years ago. I was lonely. If only I could tell you, I'm sorry.*

Kane's heart raced. This is getting worse. *I'm really losing it.* He picked up his pace until the voice faded behind him. He had always heard things but now, hearing voices from both the living and dead was getting to be over the top. Already people thought him a nutcase, but he had always pushed their comments aside. *At some point they're going to lock me up in the insane ward.* He breathed in deep and let it out, moving at a fast pace past all the other patient rooms.

A gathering of nurses talked in hushed tones as a police officer questioned each individually. He glanced over to see a pretty young nurse separated from the others and a detective writing notes down from what she was telling him. *I'll have to talk with her at some point, if I can get close enough.* Pulling out his badge and holding it up for the police officer to see, he moved past the yellow tape sectioning off the room where Jared lay. A man and woman Kane remembered to be Jared's mother and father sat next to their son, Jared, lying unmoving on his bed, the woman holding his hand. *Great. They'll be happy to see me,* Kane thought bitterly to himself when the boy's father, John, looked over to see him standing behind them. John's eyes were glistening with tears.

John turned to face him. "What the hell do you want? Shouldn't you be out talking with some dead bodies?" he asked sarcastically.

"Hello, Mr. and Mrs. Stone." Kane stepped forward, his hand outstretched to shake John's hand.

John didn't move. "It's been years and you still haven't found who did this to our boy." He nodded to his son in the bed. "And now, he almost died again. Where were you?"

"Sir, I've been searching for years for the man who hurt Jared and I have not stopped. I'm here to check on Jared. I will leave the two of you to visit with your son." He stepped back as he spoke and began to turn around before a voice stopped him in his tracks.

I'm here. Please! I'm so hungry.

CHAPTER SEVEN

Betrayal

WHAT IS GOING ON? J-Rock tried moving, but nothing would budge. Just a moment before, he had been walking down the alley with his crew to meet a new distributor of cocaine when he felt another migraine approaching. Darkness immediately followed. *Why does this keep happening to me?* he thought as he tried to move. Once again, he found himself paralyzed. It almost felt as though he were floating in some black hole with nothing to grab onto to pull himself to safety. The sounds of footsteps near him brought relief; they helped him to believe he was not dead. He smelled a fragrant perfume. *I can smell, I can hear, but I can't move.* He felt his heart pounding. *I've been in fights, I've seen people die, and this feeling is the scariest shit I've ever dealt with.* He tried to scream, but no sound would come out. At the point that he felt things couldn't get any worse, he began to feel as though he was falling. It was as though he was on a dropping carnival ride. It felt as though he had been falling for days when a jolt of pain spread from his shoulder. He moved his hand up to where the pain originated and found a sticky wet fluid. *I can move!* Relief spread through him until it occurred to him why his shoulder was wet and sticky.

The blackness that had been all around him faded and he found himself staring at the stormy night sky. He was on his back, holding his shoulder, his gun still in his back pocket. The sound of gunfire was recognizable to him and he propped himself up to look at his surroundings. His right-hand man lay lifeless next to him in a pool of his own blood, a gaping wound in the side of his head. In the distance, he could make out the colors of a rival gang. *How did they know? Someone set us up!* He looked up to see Gash, looking down at him, smiling.

"You done, ma man!" Gash brought up his gun to point it at J-Rock.

J-Rock's felt his heart rise into his throat. "Gash. What are you doing? I helped you out, man." J-Rock backed away, crawling awkwardly on the ground, his hand splashing into his friend's blood. "Why?"

Fatty was on the ground behind Gash, a gushing gunshot wound in his leg. The gang further ahead was laughing at the fat man struggling with his own weight, as he attempted to rise. Gash ignored him.

"Just business, you know that." Gash pulled back the hammer of his pistol and aimed for J-Rock's head, the gun shaking slightly.

A loud grunt came from behind Gash as the big man was now on his feet, rushing toward Gash as he turned around to face his attacker. Gunfire sounded as the gang behind Fatty fired a few shots into his back. Droplets of blood flew through the air as the bullets hit their target. Pain registered on the large man's face, but he did not falter and kept moving toward Gash. Not waiting any longer, Gash raised the gun to aim at Fatty's head and pulled the trigger. There was a sickening crack as the bullet burrowed into the man's skull. Fatty stood still a moment before collapsing, his body twitching, blood covering the ground where he had fallen. *He died for me. Move!* J-Rock reached for his gun. It was good to hold it again. He felt powerful.

Gash, hearing the noise behind him, wheeled around to face J-Rock, but was too slow. Two shots fired from the revolver in J-Rock's hand, but to J-Rock's dismay, one missed, and the other only grazed Gash's arm. J-Rock rolled to his side and rose to his knees before sprinting and ducking behind a garbage bin in the alley. Metallic sounds rang in his ears as bullets meant for him hit the metal of the garbage bin. Peering around the bin, he searched for Gash. *I'm going to kill you. If it's the last thing I do, I will kill you*, he thought as he glimpsed the man slip into an alley off to the side. The rest of the rival gang was still farther up the alley, randomly shooting at him to keep him at bay while Gash escaped. Sirens were blaring in the distance, but getting louder and louder as police were on their way to investigate the shooting. The gunfire abruptly stopped as the gang dispersed. Turning around, J-Rock saw a police cruiser stopped at the end of the alley behind him. A policeman opened the door and took cover behind it, pointing his gun at him.

"Put your gun down and your hands behind your head," the policeman shouted.

I could go down like a man. His heart raced as his finger twitched on the trigger of the gun. *I'm not ready to die. I still need to kill that shithead Gash.* Letting out a deep breath, he let the gun fall to the ground and raised his hands to his head. He wouldn't be able to put up much of a fight anyway. His head was spinning and the pain from his shoulder was becoming unbearable. Footsteps rushing toward him meant a policeman was approaching.

"On your knees!" the cop shouted.

He obeyed, but not on purpose. His vision faded. He fell to the ground, unconscious.

CHAPTER EIGHT

Recovery

"I NEED HIM TO answer some questions. He may have some important information related to a case of mine." A man's deep voice cut through the blackness.

"He needs rest. This young man has lost lots of blood. He'll recover soon enough, but you need to let him rest." Another man's voice, this one a bit higher pitched. Steady beeps sounded between the talking.

"I don't give a rat's ass how much blood he lost. Do you realize who this guy is?" the man with the deep voice demanded.

"No, I don't, and I don't really care. I'm a doctor and it's my duty to help those that need my help, regardless of their actions."

"Well, in case you do have any curiosity, he happens to be a higher-up figure with one of our city's most violent gangs. He might be able to help me nail the leader." The cop paused. "Please, wake him."

"You will have to wait, Detective Kane," the doctor replied.

"Call me when he wakes then. Immediately."

J-Rock felt the doctor checking something on his shoulder and pain shot through his body. He imagined himself moaning in agony and he thought he heard his own voice in the distance. The doctor was fidgeting with some machinery and something tugged in his arm. A numbing sensation flowed through his body. Sleep beckoned, and it relieved him to drift off away from the world and all its hardships that lay ahead for him.

***

Odd dreams filled his mind. At times he was fighting away the pain from his shoulder, but others, he found himself stuck, unable to move again. It seemed like he would bounce from one situation back to the other, neither offering any relief from the exhaustion he felt. At one point, he guessed he heard the detective's voice again, but this time he wasn't talking about him as a criminal but, instead, as a victim. Kane was talking with his parents and they actually cared about him as parents should love their kids. J-Rock hadn't talked with his parents for years now. He scared them. They hadn't wanted to know what he was doing in his spare time when he would disappear for a night and even for several days. At times, familiar voices would talk in the room. He could make out his father's voice on several occasions. Today, *Dad* had decided to check on his son again - J-Rock figured it was more likely he was looking for some tail. He tried to lash out with his arm and yell for his father to leave. It was infuriating to have to listen to the dickhead who called himself his father. He thought of all the beatings he suffered at his father's hands. *Stupid old man, shut up already! If I weren't stuck like this, I might end your stupid life once and for all!* He tried moving, and it felt as though he might be able to, but then he switched back to the pain and the beeping of the machine in the background.

Forcing his eyes open, he tried to figure out how long he'd been drifting between different worlds. It felt like hours, but it might have been days. Bright light burned into his mind. *God, my head hurts!* He raised a hand up to cover his eyes and felt the uncomfortable tug of a needle in his hand, so he put it back down. His eyes adjusted to the difference in light and he saw what appeared to be a curtain wrapped around his bed. Through a slight crack where the curtain met the wall, he saw a window, spilling light into the room. His shoulder throbbed some, but it wasn't anything he couldn't deal with. The smell of antiseptic chemicals hit him and he felt the rise of bile from his stomach. With nothing around for him to puke into, he turned to his side and heaved whatever was in his stomach to the floor.

Footsteps rushed to him and he looked up as the curtain slid open. J-Rock wiped his mouth, trying to clean himself up the best he could, when he saw a beautiful blond woman in scrubs. She rushed to help him lay back on the bed.

"Not feeling well?" she asked in a concerned voice.

J-Rock looked at the name tag to read the name, Kate. "It smells like shit in here. Made me wanna puke." He glanced down to the floor covered in his vomit. "Clean that shit up."

"The painkiller you've been on may upset your stomach," she crossed her arms, "and I'm not your personal servant. I'll get someone in here to clean it up."

She glanced over at the machine next to his bed and reviewed the readings. Satisfied with what she saw, she moved over to remove the needle from his hand. The perfume she wore helped block some of the other smells that were bothering him. She smiled at him when she saw him looking at her.

"Looks like you're doing fine. The doctor should stop by in a bit to talk with you." She let go of his arm and turned to leave.

J-Rock whistled at her. "Mmmm! Mmm! Nice ass, Kate."

"Pig. There's a cop outside your door. Careful not to drop the soap when they take you away." Kate stormed out of the room.

J-Rock pulled a pillow out from under his head and covered his face with it. *If the stupid hospital didn't smell bad enough, now I have to smell my own puke!* His stomach turned at the thought and he fought the urge to throw up once more. There was a cop outside the door. *What can they have on me? I didn't shoot anyone, or at least anyone they could prove I shot.* His mind raced, thinking of ways they might have something on him, but nothing came. *They have my gun; they might be able to match something with it, but those would be old cases.* J-Rock's heart beat faster as he imagined going to prison. If he got placed in the wrong prison with few friends, other gangs would notice his tattoos and he wouldn't last long.

"Well, Mr. J-Rock himself!" the voice from his sleep interrupted his thoughts. It was the voice of the detective.

J-Rock moved the pillow away and laughed when he saw the older man, wearing a long jacket that reminded him of the Columbo re-runs his Dad always watched. The jacket covered a suit that looked to be from the 70s, and the shirt underneath had some brown stain on it that appeared to be fresh. "What the hell do you want?" J-Rock asked.

"I've heard about some of your work on the streets and that you've helped bring in quite a lot of profit for your friends. I can nail your ass to the wall today, or we can work something out if you help me get to Slice." He stepped forward, smiling.

"No idea what you are talking about, Gramps." J-Rock turned to look out the window. It was a sunny day. *Hang in there, he doesn't have anything.* He smiled. *He's got nothing.*

"You're right, scumbag, I don't. But I will. Give me time and I will." Kane nodded at him.

"What?" J-Rock looked stunned.

"Oh, nothing."

How did he do that? I'll kill him. After I kill Gash, I'll kill him.

Kane shook his head. "Look, kid, you help me, and I'll get you out of the mess you're in." He paused a moment. "Help me get Slice, and I'll get the guy that turned on you — oh, what's his name? Gash?"

J-Rock's eyes went wide. "Get out of my room. I'm done talking to you."

"Think about it, kid. This is your chance at a decent life. Otherwise, you'll end up like your friends in the alley."

"I said get out. I'm done talking," J-Rock shouted.

Kane surged forward and hovered over J-Rock, his face peering down at him, flushed red. He appeared to be holding himself back from strangling J-Rock where he lay.

"Look, you little turd. If I had my way, I would kill you with my bare hands where you are. I really don't give a flying crap if I go to prison over it or not. The only reason I don't, is because I need to get to your boss. If you help me with this, I'll let you live in the end. If you don't – well, I'll just take you out with your boss — and I'll make sure it's as painful as possible." Kane winked and stood back, taking a deep breath as he did so.

J-Rock felt his heart pounding and his face redden. If they hadn't tied him up in this stupid hospital bed, the detective wouldn't be talking to him that way. The conversation would have ended with the old jerk sporting a bullet in his head. He tried to look calm and unshaken. "Panties in a twist, Detective?"

Kane stared back at him, exasperation written on his old face. He sighed before turning around and walking out the open door.

Stupid idiot, J-Rock shook his head. *How did he know what I was thinking? Maybe it's left over drugs in your system and you imagined it,* he laughed to himself, and a bolt of pain shot through his shoulder as he did so. His hand clasped the wound as he held his breath. *Not ready for action yet, I guess.*

A knock at the door made him jump. A man entered who he assumed must be his doctor.

"Hello, Mr. Stone. I'm your doctor." His hand reached out to shake J-Rock's. When he realized J-Rock's right arm had the wound, he quickly moved to shake his other hand, which J-Rock ignored as well. "You can call me Frank." He smiled and J-Rock thought he saw a slight wink behind the doctor's thick, smudgy glasses.

J-Rock noticed a pricey Rolex watch wrapped around the doctor's wrist. Frank must have noticed, because he moved to cover it with his shirtsleeve. Frank looked at him for a moment before speaking.

"You must work out a lot, judging by your arms. What do your tattoos represent?" Frank asked his patient in a light tone.

What the hell? This guy a fairy or what? J-Rock turned his head away to look out the window.

More footsteps approached. This time the pretty nurse, Kate, entered the room. She didn't look at him, apparently purposely avoiding his eye contact.

J-Rock watched her hips as she moved. "Hey baby! I knew you'd miss me."

Kate scowled. "Jerk!" she replied as she went about checking his pulse.

"Kate. That's not how we treat our patients!" Frank's tone had changed from light and sweet to deep and angry. "You keep up with that attitude and I'll make sure to give your new job to someone who deserves it — not some girl who acts like she should be home knitting sweaters and popping out babies." He looked down to J-Rock and winked.

J-Rock clenched his fists as his temper flared. With a burst of speed, he swung his good hand around to clasp the doctor's throat. Kate jumped back and Frank tried to move away, but he was too slow. The strong young man's grip tightened around the front of the doctor's neck. Frank gasped for air and clenched J-Rock's wrist.

"PLEA-!" Frank tried his best to speak, but no words escaped.

Kate grabbed J-Rock's arm, trying to pull it away from the doctor, but his grip was much too strong.

"Help!" she yelled out as she scratched at J-Rock's arm with her nails, drawing blood.

J-Rock looked at the woman clawing at his arm. "Stop it, bitch, or you're next!" His face was hot with rage and he was at his tipping point, which was never good. Whenever he lost control, he'd hurt people beyond his original intentions.

The sound of someone running through the doorway broke through the noise of the doctor struggling to gain his breath. J-Rock looked into the doctor's eyes. They were wide with shock and fear. It was getting harder for the man to keep his lids open.

"Listen up, Frank. I just met you and I don't like you. I don't like the way you're treating my woman." He looked over to Kate, still struggling to free the doctor. His arm was raw from the scratches he had received. She looked surprised at his comment. J-Rock smiled and winked at her before turning back to the doctor. "I can end your miserable life right now, you faggot."

"Let the doctor go!" a policeman shouted from behind the doctor. His nightstick was out and raised into the air, ready to beat down on J-Rock's arm.

J-Rock smiled at all the people gathered around the bed and let his grip go. Frank sunk to the ground, clutching his throat and gasping for air. Kate rushed to the doctor's side to check if he needed any medical attention. The cop cuffed J-Rock to the rail of the bed before checking on the doctor as well. J-Rock laughed out loud as the cop and Kate helped the doctor to his feet and escorted him out of the room. *Well, good luck getting away with that, you idiot!* It was good to lash out and release a little frustration, though. *At least the little twinkle toes won't be batting his eyes at me anymore.*

CHAPTER NINE

Mama Shayga

KANE LEFT THE HOSPITAL feeling as though there was no chance the kid would ever speak out against Slice. *Can you blame him?* he thought to himself, knowing that the gang leader had so many followers who respected and feared him. Slice would make it a priority to kill anyone who might step forward to help police track him down. There had been a few such instances, and before the police had a chance to talk to any witnesses, they'd wind up in a ditch. The victims always had deep slices from a knife etched into their skin. Even more unnerving, unrelated to the case was his own vision. When the boy had wound up in the hospital after the gang fight, Kane had seen what appeared to be a dark fog leave the boy's body. Shortly after, another form of the fog, this one white, took its place. He knew he'd never get anything out of Jared with his interrogation, but was more curious about the fog he had seen the day before. Relieved that he had not seen the same sort of unexplainable event, he was still unnerved by what he has seen this time: a darkish glow had radiated from the boy. *Heart attack?* he stopped at his car and checked his pulse. *I'm not short of breath. Heart attack would be nice. I guess it's just insanity.* The door to his car squeaked as he opened it and the shocks grunted from his weight when he sat down. "Old and squeaky like me," he said out loud to himself as he closed the door and started the car.

Before heading home for the evening, Kane made his way to a poor section of the city. The sights switched from shiny buildings and pretty parks to decrepit factories long left vacant. Run-down apartment buildings added to the scenery. Women lined the streets waiting for a seedy businessman to pick them up, as did men dressed as women. Some waved to him and smiled. Kane knew some. Not from picking them up for pleasure, but because he would offer money and food from time to time for information. The amount of information street workers collected always amazed him. All it took was a little generosity, and the gossip provided might be the key to nailing a criminal's ass to the wall. Arriving at his destination, he pulled the car up to the side of the road, turning off the engine before getting out.

The air reeked of decay and smog. Decay from the trash and filth in the streets and smog from the city the air that would be carried far to waft down the suburban streets. An alley stood in front of him, littered with trash and makeshift hovels comprising cardboard or whatever else a desperate person could find. Ragged-looking people lay inside the hovels or slept, covered in newspapers, on the ground. Kane walked down the alley, ignoring people tugging at his pants, begging for change. The putrid aroma of human waste stung his nose, and he held his breath for a moment, hoping the next breath would be more pleasant. He looked around and his heart sank at the people he saw, all devoid of hope, having given up on life long ago. An old lady sat against a brick wall, shivering. *She'll be dead soon*, he thought to himself as he walked past her. Police would often come through the alley and carry out the dead bodies of those that had grown too weak to survive the cold nights. Kane made it a priority to help at least one person out a year. He'd love to do more, but he only had so much money and he needed to live himself.

Tarps stood ahead at the end of the alley, shaped in the form of a large tent. He stopped outside the small opening.

"Mama Shayga. It's Kane," he hollered.

"Kane! I thought you'd be coming soon nuff!" an older woman's raspy voice echoed back. "Well, git on in here."

Pulling back the flaps, Kane stepped into the tent. Clutter was strewn across the ground and the inside reeked of a body that had not showered in months. Kane tried his best not to gag at the awful stench, but it was too much and he began coughing. An older woman sat on an overturned bucket, staring at him with a grin showing two upper teeth, the only ones she had left. Covered in various articles of clothing, it was hard to tell how big or small she was. Mama Shayga pointed to another bucket turned upside down for him to sit.

"Take a load off dose achin' feet, Shuga Kane." She laughed and looked proud of herself and her joke.

Kane walked over to the bucket and brushed off what he hoped was dirt before sitting. Mama reached down to the floor, picking up a plastic cover with pieces of what appeared to have been a sandwich, pulled apart. She held the food out to Kane. *God knows what trash bin that came out of,* Kane thought to himself and smiled, shaking his head.

"No thanks, Mama."

"No no no. I know you be hungry. Must eat to be strong, Shuga." She shook the plate a little for him to take a piece.

Kane reached over and grabbed a piece of sandwich and held it a moment, hoping it would please her and she'd stop pushing for him to eat. Instead, she stared at him, waiting and smiling. Reluctantly, he raised the sandwich to his lips and she nodded at him. *If I expect to talk with her at all, I have to do it.* His stomach turned. Slowly, he nibbled the edge of the bread.

"Not how strong boys eat t'all. Uh uh. No no." Mama shook her head in disgust.

In one quick motion, Kane crammed the stale bread and aged meat with cheese in his mouth, chewing as little as possible, and swallowed. He held his breath a moment, trying to avoid the aftertaste that was sure to hit him. Mama jumped up, overturning the pail she was sitting on, and bounced around the tent, hopping up and down, laughing. Pieces of loose clothing fell to the ground as she hopped from one foot to the other. Kane rolled his eyes. Once Mama Shayga got into a fit like this, it was always a guess when she'd come back to reality. A minute passed before she put the bucket back and sat down, still smiling. Her eyes were watery from her laughing fit.

"You ate that gunk? You one weirdo, Shuga. Strange strange strange. Mmmm hmmm." She nodded and then stopped suddenly, sticking her finger in her ear, wiggling before talking again. "Dunno where I got that meat, but if you fine after a few, then I'll eat." She slapped her hands down on her knees and laughed again. "Weirdo weirdo weirdo Shuga!" As abruptly as she started laughing she stopped. Her smile disappeared, replaced with a serious and concerned look. "Kane, I know why you are here. I saw it in my sleep."

Kane frowned, thinking about how the woman's head worked. If you were able to get past her odd behaviors, Mama Shayga tended to be helpful. Kane's mouth tasted horrible and he felt like vomiting. Instead he cleared his throat.

"Mama, what did you see?" he asked.

She smiled. "I saw you, dear. I saw you and the other you. Two of you there are. Two of him there are, one good, one bad, all because of a decision when the time lines were close."

"What do you mean? I don't understand." He stared back at her, perplexed.

"And you think I do, Kane? I eat from trash cans and sit on and dance around plastic buckets, you dolt."

Kane smiled at her. "Mama, I've been seeing and hearing things," he paused a moment, "well, more than usual. I saw light around someone today."

"Every person is a shell, and inside the shell lies our energy or our spirit. Visualizing a spirit outside the body means the person's spirit is not contained. The disconnected spirit can wander, or even get lost." She reached out and touched Kane's hand. "Kane, every decision in one's life causes branches to extend. New worlds formed with each decision. Our visions are from where our world's time line is crossing with another's. This should only happen once in awhile. I'm afraid we are too close to another time line, allowing for our worlds to mix. Our branches must veer in another direction. Until then, spirits may get trapped in worlds they don't belong in."

Kane took a deep breath and exhaled. "That tells me nothing, Mama. What am I to do with any of that?"

"For our world, there is the other, based on a decision. There is you here and you there, both the same. You need to find whose decision made our world. That person will be the only complete opposite between the two worlds."

Kane shook his head. "Then what? Do some voodoo dance?"

"No idea, Kane, sorry. I only know that our worlds should not be mixing as they are. I do not know what will happen if they continue to do so."

"I still don't und—" he stopped in mid sentence. Mama Shayga's eyes glazed over and she stared into the distance.

Her eyes darted back to him and she smiled from ear to ear. "Shuga Kane! Hungry? Eat eat eat!" she reached down and picked up the plate of stale sandwich. "Big boys need full tumtums!" she shook the makeshift plate at him.

She's gone again. No more from her today. Kane shook his head "no" and stood. "Not today, Mama. Looks delicious though."

Mama stood up and started to step forward to push him back down to sit. Kane managed to avoid her reaching arms and exited the tent. *Sad. A crazy, homeless, old lady is the only person who understands me.* A strange end to the day, and Kane had been through enough. He started the car and began his commute to his empty home.

CHAPTER TEN

Hope

"Nurse!" Jared heard the man his parents were trying to shoo out of the room yell. "Nurse! I think your patient needs help!"

Footsteps rushed to his room.

"Just what the hell are you doing now?" John asked.

"I think your son may need help. I don't think he's as comatose as you believe him to be. Please! Trust me."

Jared could hear a chair skidding across the floor as his father stood up. "What? Another vision? I'm warning you, Detective. Get out!" John's voice boomed, filled with hatred.

Dad! Please. I am here. Jared almost felt as if his eyes were moving behind his closed lids.

"John, please. Calm down," Lana spoke through her tears.

A cool hand touched his arm and Jared could smell a flowery perfume. Kate had come to see if he was OK. "His pulse is beating much faster. Did he do something, Detective? What happened?"

"I, well, it's hard to expla-" the detective's gruff voice began. John's voice cut off the detective's.

"Hard to explain? It was a stupid vision, wasn't it?"

"No, no, not really. More like him talking in his mind. I happened to," Kane cleared his throat, "I happened to hear it."

Jared heard the sounds of a scuffle and someone fall to the floor. John's voice followed, "I'm sick of you! You told us you'd help us and you've done nothing but torment us. You and your damned visions." John spat.

"John, you didn't have to hit him," Lana spoke out and Jared heard the click of her heels on the floor. Jared could hear her helping the detective get to his feet.

"No, it's fine Mrs. Stone. I know I'm a bit hard to take at times," Kane said.

"No, not just a bit hard to take. How a damned nutcase can get to be a detective, I don't know. What the hell is the world coming to?" John's footsteps sounded, as though he were pacing back and forth across the room.

"Mr. Stone, if you don't cool down, I'll call for help." Kate's voice was stern. "Detective Kane, are you OK?"

"Oh, I'm used to events like that by now," he said.

"I'm surprised you didn't see it coming with all your powers." John wouldn't let go.

"John, please. Enough!" Lana's voice sounded angry.

Kate leaned forward and the smell of her perfume was stronger now. She put her hand on his forehead. "Jared, if you can hear me, can you move in some way to show us you are there?"

This is my only chance. The thought burned inside of him. He lashed out with all his might, and to his surprise, his arm jerked. Kate stepped back to avoid his thrashing arm. *Can't have missed that!*

"What just happened?" John sounded shocked.

"He moved, John! Jared moved!" Lana stood up and gave him a hug.

The atmosphere of the room changed in a flash. Jared heard the sounds of his parents shouting with joy between fits of crying. Pangs of hunger stormed through Jared's stomach. *Please, please, I'm so hungry.*

Kane's voice came from behind the noise of his parents. "I think your son may be hungry."

"Yes, he most likely is. It has been some time since he's had any nutrients. May I reinstall the equipment, Mr. and Mrs. Stone?" Kate asked.

Jared thrashed again. *Please! Help me!*

"Yes, please do it now," John replied.

Jared felt a wave a relief flow through him. He would not have to face the terrible hunger pains any longer. But he also knew that he was not yet safe. It was exhausting to fight the urge to drift off into the dark again. He had hope now, though, and Kate was out there to keep him from drifting.

Chapter Eleven

An Eye Opener

Jared didn't know how long it had been since the machines had started working again. Kate would visit him every day, as would his parents. They would all talk to him and ask him to move this or that body part, on which he would focus with all his might. Sometimes he'd hear them clap and laugh. Other times he'd hear, "Ah, that's OK Jared. You're doing great."

The door to his room opened and he heard Kate's footsteps. *Has it been a night already? Wasn't she just here?* It felt as though he had just finished trying to move all day.

"Jared. It's me, Kate."

He loved the sound of her voice. It was almost music to his ears. *I wonder how she looks. I bet she's beautiful.* The thought made him want to open his eyes, but it was useless. No matter how hard he tried, he could not break through whatever fog was there in his way. *Or, I'll open my eyes and she'll be a 70-year-old grandma.* He laughed to himself at that thought. *No, I bet she's beautiful.* She touched his arm; he loved it when she did that.

"Jared, I know you must be tired from all the hard work today, but I also know that you can do this. Open your eyes and come back. I'd love to meet you." She gave his arm a gentle squeeze.

I want to. I do! But I can't. He felt tears form at the thought. *Tears? I have tears? If I have tears, then I should be able to open my eyes, right?* He tried, but nothing. *Wait, she said she's here after-hours? Why?*

Almost as if she heard him ask, she responded, "I'm sorry, Jared. I'll leave you alone. I only thought we could try once more today. You are so close to beating this. Your parents love you. You are lucky to have such a loving family." She paused. "I never knew my parents. My mother had me when she was young and put me up for adoption. My foster parents were nice, but were never close. They had a child shortly after they took me in, so I was always second in their eyes. A family that loves their child so much should not have to suffer as yours do. You should not have to suffer either. Life can be so unfair."

Jared moved his arm a little to try to reach out to her. She didn't seem to notice.

"I don't know why I'm telling you this — I feel so stupid. I guess I needed someone to talk to. Sad that my best friend is in a coma and doesn't even know me." She laughed quietly but loud enough for him to hear. She squeezed his arm once more before standing up and taking a deep breath. "OK, I'll let you rest. Tomorrow is another day. We will get you out of this so you can get the bastards that did this to you. Detective Kane seems like a good man. A bit weird, but good."

She turned to leave and began to walk away from the bed. *Come on Jared, snap the hell out of it!* Jared focused his energy on his eyes. Like two iron gates, his eyelids lifted. Light burned through his head as he saw the room that had been his prison for years. It surprised him that the room was dark. The only light spilled in from the outside street lamp. His eyes hurt at having to adjust to even such a small amount of light. He looked around as best he could, but he still couldn't turn his head. In the darkness, he could see Kate's outline walking to the door of his room. Jared tried to move his lips.

"Kate!" he gasped, and to his amazement, the sound escaped his lips.

Kate stopped and turned around to see her patient looking at her from across the room. "Jared? You opened your eyes!" She jumped slightly, emphasizing her excitement.

She turned on the light to the room and it blinded him. "Light!" Jared moaned.

"Sorry!" she turned the light back off and rushed over to his bed.

"Water," Jared cried out. His throat was dry; his mouth felt like it was full of sand.

Kate rushed to the sink in the room and filled a cup with water. She tried not to spill any as she ran back and lifted Jared's head to drink from it. The water felt good as it traveled down his throat. He finished the entire cup and Kate let his head down to the pillow. Exhausted, Jared's eyes closed as he began to drift off to sleep. *Tomorrow will be a big day*, he thought to himself as sleep overtook him.

Chapter Twelve

Freedom

"Jared Stone!" the cop's voice echoed through the halls of the jail. The year for the aggravated assault sentence for attacking the doctor was up and he was free to go. J-Rock laughed to himself as he stood up from sitting on the lower bed. Jim, the other resident of the room, smiled at him. Jim was a big, muscular man, with identical gang tattoos as himself. J-Rock clapped him on the back as he walked to the door of his cell. J-Rock had been lucky to be placed with a member of his own gang and not in one with any of his rivals. If it had been one of them, neither would have left captivity. One would likely be dead, the other forced to serve more time for killing his cellmate.

"I'll see you on the outside, bro!" J-Rock flashed the gang signal as he said goodbye to the other man. He doubted he'd ever see him again; he knew the man was in for killing a rival gang member. Jim was waiting for his court date, but J-Rock was sure that the court would deem Jim guilty and send him to prison. J-Rock was glad he didn't have to face Jim in a fight. The man could pummel him into mush. *Probably had enough steroids in his system to turn his balls into peas*, he thought to himself as the guard opened the door.

The door clanged as it slid to let him walk out. J-Rock looked at the guard as he passed him by. The man appeared weak and out of shape, his stomach hanging over his belt. J-Rock smirked at him and shook his head in disgust. The guard closed the door behind him.

"Free to go for now, kid." The guard pointed toward the exit at the end of the hallway where there was a door with a small, closed window. "But I'm sure I'll see that rotten face of yours again. You guys always come back."

J-Rock began walking to the door; his anger, as usual, was beginning to burn inside him. *Keep it cool, man. If I screw up now, I'll be right back in the cell and maybe off to prison.*

"Yo, Fat-ass! No disrespect for my brother!" Jim hollered from behind them as they walked away.

The guard, sensing the anger rising in J-Rock, kept pressing. "Oh, I see. You like the big men. Lots of big men like your friend waiting where you'll end up." He snorted as he laughed. "Jim gave it to you good, did he?"

It's all a trick. He's trying to make me snap. J-Rock clenched his jaw and clutched his fists until his knuckles cracked as he kept walking. He was halfway down the hallway now. Other incarcerated people watched as he walked past their cells. Some cheered, seeing a fellow inmate getting his freedom. Others swore at or harassed him. J-Rock stopped mid-stride. He envisioned a checklist:

1) Grab fat prick by his neck.

2) Slam fat prick's head into the cell door.

3) Listen to fat prick's skull crack.

4) Repeat steps 2 & 3.

5) Admire bloody mess and brain bits in the paint.

The guard prodded him with his nightstick. "You got a problem, son? Let's talk about it. I'd love to chat with you. Show me what you got." He poked him once more.

J-Rock's mind spun. Snapping the man's neck wouldn't be a hardship at all. It would feel so nice. His face flushed. *I'm losing control. Keep cool.* He looked at the door straight ahead of him. It seemed to fade as his rage subsided. *One step, two steps, three steps.* He counted to himself as he moved forward. It wasn't that far away now. He could make out the guard standing on the other side of the door, through the window.

"You're all talk when you have a gun. Not so tough now, are you? You dumbass gang kids are all the same." The guard was beside him now.

The guard's fatty hand gripped J-Rock's arm tightly. It made it worse that the hand was slimy with perspiration. *If I ever see you again, you're a dead man,* J-Rock thought. With every step, J-Rock's anticipation mounted; the door was directly in front of him now. The guard waved to the man on the other side of the door and a buzzer sounded, followed by a loud click. With a creak, the door swung open. Cool air swished past his face. Still holding his arm, the guard stepped through the door with him.

J-Rock felt the guard let go of his hold on him. He gathered his belongings and exited to the lobby. Detective Kane stood near the door, watching him. *Another one on my list.* He shook his head as he approached the detective.

"This is your last chance, J-Rock. I can help you get out of the mess you're in. You can live a normal life." Kane stood in front of him, blocking the exit.

"You're in my way, old man." J-Rock stopped to face the detective, his chin raised so he was looking down at him. J-Rock was about a foot taller than Kane. The detective didn't move. J-Rock took a step forward and his chest was up against the older man's. "You want to die today?"

Kane stood still a moment before holding a card up in front of the younger man's face. "If you wise up, this is how you can reach me."

J-Rock swatted the card away and it fell to the floor. Kane backed away and J-Rock walked past, bumping him with his shoulder as he did so. *If only I could shove a gun up his ass and pull the trigger!* Unable to lash out at the stupid detective, he slammed into the door. The iron door was the last thing standing between him and his freedom. It swung open with a crash and the light from the outside blinded him. A warm breeze blew his hair back. The sidewalk radiated heat. It felt good to be outdoors again. J-Rock smiled, hearing the sounds of the city.

A man wearing J-Rock's gang colors stood beside a parked car and motioned to him. J-Rock spat on the concrete sidewalk. He could almost hear the saliva sizzle as it hit the ground. He grinned at the other man and walked to where he waited. *I'm dead if they think I ratted,* he thought, sending a chill of warning through his body. Instinctively he reached into his bag for the reassurance of his gun, but it was gone. The cops had taken it after the shooting. J-Rock's heart pounded faster. *Why would they send someone out for me?* He eyed the man waiting for him, sized him up. He was smaller than J-Rock. *If they wanted me dead, they would have sent more than one person. They'd want to ensure the job got done without any snags.* He felt a little more confident as he analyzed the situation. If it came down to a physical struggle, he decided that he'd be more than a match for the smaller man.

"Get in. Slice wants to talk wid ya." The man didn't wait for a response.

Slice? Oh shit. This is either really good or REALLY bad. J-Rock's heart raced again. He had seen Slice only once in his time with the gang and he had never actually spoken with him. Slice liked to keep a limited circle of people close to him. If he wanted to see someone in the gang, it meant one of two things: either reward for a good job, or punishment in the form of execution. The last person J-Rock had known to visit Slice reportedly stashed away drug money, and the money, of course, belonged to the gang's account. His body turned up hanging upside down in a back alley, empty of blood from all the slices he had taken from a sharp blade. Each slice was made slowly and spread out over t ime.

J-Rock walked to the passenger door and opened it. The smell of old weed smoke wafted out. Swallowing his fear, he sat down in the seat next to the driver. The driver sped off before J-Rock even had a chance to close the door. J-Rock reached out, pulling the door shut just before it would have hit a nearby sign post.

"Shit, man! What's the hurry?" J-Rock slammed his hand onto the dash to emphasize his frustration. "You want me to fall out?"

The other man ignored his outburst.

"So what's your name?" J-Rock asked.

"X," the other man said. He looked over at J-Rock and smiled. The few teeth still in place were black.

J-Rock nodded. He knew him now. X was Slice's main drug man. He had gotten his name for his dependency on Ecstasy. He was also crazy — most likely due to his need for a steady high.

"Now shut up, foo. Slice dunt like to wait."

X turned away from him, focusing on his driving. The car sped up and they began passing cars on the freeway. It wasn't long until they were back into the gang's territory. X sped a little faster now. Cops didn't bother many of the gang in this area. They knew that roughing up gang members alone meant a shortened lifespan. J-Rock's mind raced at the thought of what would happen when he was face to face with Slice.

Chapter Thirteen

Bubble Gum and Visions

Well, that didn't go well at all. Kane shook his head as he watched J-Rock walk to the car. *I tried.* He released a breath of air as he thought, *Yeah, I tried, but I gotta stop kidding myself. I don't give a rat's ass about that punk. It's Slice that I'm after — and he's still a ghost.* Kane bent down to pick up the card that was lying on the floor. A pop sounded from behind him, and he felt it more than he heard it. "God, you old fart," he told himself. He reached back to rest a hand where his back had cracked and tried to stand up straight. A laugh distracted him. A younger man — a security guard — stood off to his left, snickering at him. Even here, Kane had a reputation for being nuts. *Laugh all you want, kid. You won't be laughing when that heart attack hanging over your head introduces itself.* It was the first thing Kane saw when he looked at the young man with the smirk across his face. One minute he was jogging, and the next, clutching his chest. Alone, he would thrash on the cold cement of the sidewalk. Darkness would surround him and his time would be over.

The security guard who had let J-Rock out was watching Kane from a distance. The guard waved to him. Kane had known Steve for all his time working on the police force. Steve had started with him in the beginning of Kane's career, but later discovered he wasn't cut out for the pressures of being a policeman. As soon as a position opened within the jail, Steve took the new role. Kane always made it a point to visit him when he needed to stop by the jail for any reason. He smiled and waved back.

"Kane! Been a while!" Steve held out his hand to shake Kane's. His belly shook as he spoke.

"Too long, Steve." Kane shook his hand.

He nodded. "I tried, Kane. I used all the tricks up my sleeve. He wouldn't break." He stopped as a buzzer sounded and another inmate walked to freedom.

Kane clapped him on the shoulder. "I know you did, Steve. Thanks for trying."

Steve nodded. "Anytime. I hope you're not attached to that boy. He's no good."

"No. No, he's not." Kane turned to watch the latest inmate leave to re-enter society. "I only hoped to keep him with you guys longer. I needed information from him."

"He's a firecracker ready to explode. He's also smart. If we don't see him here again, he'll probably move up in the gang. At least until he winds up dead." Steve motioned to someone behind the door that he'd be back in a minute.

Kane nodded his head in agreement. "One of these days, I will get that leader of theirs and bring him down."

"Or someone else will. You don't even know if he's still out there, Kane. Let it go. Stop wasting your time on punks like J-Rock."

Kane frowned. "This...Slice. He's ruined a lot of people's lives. I'm going to nail his ass." He tapped the other man on the arm. "Thanks again, Steve. I'll see you later." Kane turned to leave.

"Kane. Be careful. That J-Rock kid is bad news and I think we both pissed him off."

Kane nodded and made his way to where he'd parked his car. The air was heavy with humidity. He hated humidity. As he walked, his conversation with Mama Shayga nagged him. *What the hell did she mean about the two worlds? What the hell does it have to do with what I saw?* He stopped a moment and watched the traffic. Mama Shayga had led him astray in the past. Yet, there was usually some useful information in the gibberish she would provide. *She said that I need to find the person whose decision made this world.* He laughed and shook his head at the idea that he was actually giving it any mental energy. Mama Shayga had been off her rocker for a long time. If he were to start listening to her, that meant he was on his way too. *But what the hell was that light around the boy? And why did it change like that?* The squeal of a car's aging brakes broke his train of thought. He lifted his foot, and it felt as though there was some strange weight pulling it back down. Looking down, he saw the stringy pinkish substance clinging stubbornly to his foot. It appeared to be a healthy gob of Bubble Yum.

"Son of a B—" Kane stopped when he heard the laughter of a young girl. She was sitting on a bench waiting for the bus. "This your gum?" he asked her as he pointed to the gunk sticking to the bottom of his shoe.

The girl giggled.

He frowned. "When an adult asks you a question, you answer in a polite tone."

"Grumpy Frumpy!" she stuck her tongue out at him.

Kane walked over to where she sat. His shoe made clicking noises with each step he took, and small pink circles dotted each step in the cement. He reached into his pocket for his wallet and badge. He loved to put bratty kids in their place. Usually flashing the police badge did the trick. He paused before pulling the wallet out, his hand still in his jacket. The girl was not alive.

This wasn't the first time he had encountered a spirit. *Lost between realms and probably not aware she's dead*, he thought. It was always sad to see a trapped soul. The back of the bench was visible through the girl's body. A flicker rippled through her and an instant later, the bench was empty. She'd wind up sitting on the same bench another day, repeating her time at this place over and over again. Most people would not notice her. They lacked the gift Kane had. He sat on the bench where the girl had been. His feet ached and he felt trapped. Slice always managed to be one step ahead of him.

Kane sat on the bench alone for some time before standing. The gum was still stuck to his foot. At least the gum was real. He brought his focus back to J-Rock and tracking down Slice. J-Rock had some role to play in all the visions he was having. *He might be able to lead me to Slice*, he thought. "Two birds with one stone." Kane smiled and clicked his way to the car.

CHAPTER FOURTEEN

Baby Steps

EACH DAY WAS EXHAUSTING. The first challenge was trying to wake up and open his eyes in the morning. Over time, Jared found that task became easier. The harder tasks, such as moving his limbs, came next. Kate would check on him each day after his visits with the physical therapist. Often, she'd find Jared lying in bed coated with sweat and too exhausted to eat.Kate would stop by to scrub him down, which always embarrassed him. It wasn't that he didn't like it; it was great to have the dirt and sweat wiped away from his body. However, to have a beautiful woman cleaning him was incredibly awkward. *Well, at least it's not Mom,* he laughed to himself at the thought.

Kate was always professional when she gave him his sponge baths. She would make sure to cover him for the most part. She would talk to him to try and get his mind off not being able to clean himself yet. They would talk about events that Jared had missed while being in a coma. It amazed him how much life had passed him by. He had missed all of his high school years. As she would run the sponge across his skin, he would try to focus on serious thoughts. The smell of her perfume teased him.

Her hand would sometimes accidentally brush his skin and he'd try to act like it didn't happen. She would apologize and smile at him. As time progressed, it seemed as though she would slip a little more each day. Jared didn't mind; it was nice to have her so close. Kate had become his only friend, and they would often joke with one another. Jared would try his hardest to get her to laugh. It seemed to him that her whole face would light up when she smiled.

When he wasn't completing his exercises, time went by slowly. He would either listen to audio books or his family would visit with him. It amazed him to realize how much everyone cared for him. It made him sad to think about how long his recovery was taking. The doctor would share Jared's progress with his family, and he could see the disappointment in his father's eyes. It seemed his father was expecting a faster recovery from his son.

Jared lay in bed, and for the moment, he had a break with no one else in the room with him. He loved having visitors, or Kate, to talk to, but it was nice to have a moment alone to relax. He lay with his head propped up in order to watch the local news. *I can't take this anymore.* A tear streamed down his cheek to land on the pillow. *I need to move!* He was physically exhausted, but so tired of his helplessness. The therapist had been able to get him out of bed earlier, able to stand on his feet, but only with a lot of help. Jared was proud of himself, though; he had achieved a major feat.

Fighting his fatigue, he summoned whatever energy he had left. He threw his left leg over the side of the bed, where he let it dangle for a moment. His leg free of the blanket that once covered it, it was nice to feel the cool air on his skin. *OK, that's one.* With a grunt, he swung the other leg around and righted himself to sit. *Nice. I can do this!* Jared breathed in deep and pushed himself off the edge of the bed to stand on his feet. As his weight shifted, he stretched his arms out for balance. He expected a tumble to the floor, but to his relief, he stood in place.

"Alright. I've got this!" he said out loud and laughed.

Excitement rushed through his body. His legs burned from using overworked muscles. Jared focused on the exhilaration of standing and tried to ignore the pain. He fought the urge to reach out for support as he put one foot out for his first step. His memories of walking, before the accident, felt like only a day ago. It felt odd how unbalanced he was now. Moving his legs was so difficult, yet his mind felt it should not be.

His leg trembled in the air and he set his foot down on the floor. He could feel his upper body shift, but he was able to keep his balance. Jared put more weight down on his other leg to step forward. *OK, now or never*, he thought as he lifted his other foot off the floor.

Just as he thought he had stepped on his own, the leg holding most of his weight gave out. Pain radiated from his leg and he cried out in shock as gravity weighed down on him. He reached out in a panic for the bed, but only could grab the loose sheet. The cold hospital floor rushed up to meet him and the side of his face crashed against it. A strange thud echoed through his mind. Jared's vision blackened and a streak of light flashed in his eyes.

When his vision returned, he realized he lay sprawled on the floor. His cheek throbbed and his legs were so exhausted he could not muster the energy to move. *I must look like some kind of moron lying here like a dead fish*. He was at least able to shift himself so that he was lying on his back. The taste of blood made him cringe. In his fall, he had somehow bitten his cheek. He stared up at the ceiling. He thought about how much he had stared at the same ceiling since waking from his coma. It had become a game to him to count all the little holes in the panels. It would be a good two or three hours before someone would check on him. The time span between nurse visits had increased over the past couple weeks since he had begun to be able to take care of himself more and more. The floor was cold against his back and he felt the muscles in his lower back ache.

"Got yourself into a mess," he said out loud as he reached around to pull the sheet to cover himself. He wanted to cry, but pushed it aside. He had been able to get out of bed and stand up on his own. Maybe he couldn't walk, but he could stand. That was something!

Thinking time would fly by much faster if he were able to sleep, he closed his eyes. He tried to ignore the throbbing coming from his cheek. It made him wonder how bad he'd look in the morning. His mind raced. He'd never be able to sleep. Images of Kate rushed through his mind. He had only seen her in her nursing scrubs, but she was still beautiful. Jared felt as though he had been stabbed in the heart at the thought that she had no interest in him. Why would she? What on earth could he give her? Young, never completed high school, and unable to walk. He had nothing to offer.

OK, sleep isn't an option. He opened his eyes. It was too painful to think that Kate didn't feel for him the same way he did for her. He stared up at the ceiling and the little holes in the panels. *One, Two, Three, Four.........*

CHAPTER FIFTEEN

Slum Lord Payback

KATE DROVE ALONG THE trash-littered road in front of her apartment building. Finding a vacant parking spot was hopeless. She'd have to park further away. Never a good situation. This section of the city was not known for being the safest, but it was the only section close to her work that she could afford. Shaking her head, she continued past her apartment to the next street. Able to find a spot, she drove her old Ford Escort up next to an old Chevy station wagon. Shifting into reverse, the sound of the gears grinding made her cringe. The car hated reverse. One of these days, the gearbox would fall to the ground. A rough group of men nearby laughed at her. One let out a whistle at her and gestured with his hips what he was thinking about. *Pigs.* She turned back to her parking and tried to ignore the audience.

Kate parked the car in the small space with relative ease. Her car was not the prettiest or the newest, but being small, it was at least easy to park. She pulled out a can of mace from the glove compartment in case her fan club got to be too friendly. She removed the faceplate to her radio.

"I've got enough troubles; I don't need to replace this again," she told herself as she put the faceplate in her purse. She tried not to look back at the group of men. No need to give them any unintended attention. She opened the door to her car and stepped out into the street.

"Hey there sweet thang! I got something you might like," one of the men yelled, followed by his friends' laughter.

Kate didn't turn to look, but instead walked up the street. She sensed their gaze on her as she walked away.

"Oh, don't be like that! You know you want it!" the man called back again; this time his voice sounded fainter.

Kate let out a deep breath. It didn't sound as though they were following her. Trash cans full of stale garbage lined the street. Kate put her head down to cover the rotting trash odor with her own perfume.

The door to the apartment building was ajar. Light spilled out onto the cement steps. Kate rolled her eyes. *Nice security*, she thought as she walked up the steps. The main reason she had chosen this particular apartment building was for the security keypad. Only those with an access code could open the entry door. She opened the door and stepped through into the dark hallway. The hall was drab with a long stairway winding up the building. The building did have an elevator, but it has been out of order for a long time. A baby's cry shrieked through the walls. Pots and pans clamored. A loud and boisterous man's voice commanded a woman to shut the baby up. "God, I have to get out of here," Kate said out loud to herself.

First taking a deep breath, she began her long climb up the stairs to the top floor. She hated having to climb the stairs each day, but welcomed the exercise. The air seemed to be thicker and heavy with the heat rising from the units on the lower floors. Pausing a moment to catch her breath, she wiped away sweat on her forehead. She fumbled for her keys. Just as her hand brushed the keys in her purse, she noticed a lock bolt on the door.

"Son of a b—" she yelled as she hit the door. Someone had taped a note to the door which she ripped down to read.

"Payment past due. Come by the office to settle up.
Big T"

Kate crumpled the paper and wanted to cry. *This is all I need!* She had been paying small amounts on her rent weekly. Kate hoped the landlord would have a little compassion.

"Stupid, stupid girl," Kate mumbled about herself as she shook her head and threw the paper to the floor. She could have made more money working as a hospital nurse but wanted to work more with long-term patients. Kate felt that hospital nurses didn't get the opportunity to help the patients. Instead, she had opted for a lower-paying job. She could help people after the hospital brought them to a stable condition. Unfortunately, what she preferred to do for work didn't pay the bills. Kate wiped away the tears in her eyes and looked around the hallway. *Well, looks like I don't have a choice. I'll try and work something out and then look for a different position.* The thought bothered her, but she had no other choice now. Swallowing her pride, she walked down the stairs to where the landlord lived.

The air felt better lower in the building where it wasn't so stuffy. Kate hated dealing with the landlord, Big T, as he liked to call himself. She had no idea why he liked that name, but never wanted to find out either. Big T was a pig.

Hesitating a moment outside his door, Kate worked up the nerve to deal with him. *Just work out a payment deal for the last time. That's all.* Kate wiped her eyes one more time and cleared her throat before knocking on the door.

"Who's there?" Big T's muffled voice came from behind the door.

"Kate. I'm on the top floor. You left a note," Kate yelled back.

Footsteps approached the door, followed by a click as the lock released. The door swung open to show Big T, his belly busting out from his undershirt. The smell of sweat and greasy food made Kate want to gag, but she kept it back. He was dressed in his usual attire, a stained sleeveless tank top and dirty jeans.

"Kate. You owe me some money." Big T smiled, his plaque-stained teeth adding to the man's unattractiveness.

"Yes, I'm sorry—"she paused, she wouldn't say 'Big T'—"sir. I've been struggling a bit, but I will get it to you."

Big T nodded and his demeanor changed, becoming amazingly pleasant. "Kate, I understand. Times are hard."

Kate frowned in confusion. "You do?"

"Sure I do. Come on in and have some dinner with me," said Big T, smiling at her as he beckoned for her to enter. "I'm making some spaghetti and I have enough for two."

This isn't right. Leave now. Kate shook her head "no" and stepped back. "No thank you, sir. I've troubled you enough. I will get my next payment to you as soon as I am able."

Big T laughed; his belly shook with the exertion. "You OWE me money! You think you can just walk out?"

Kate didn't like where this conversation was heading and turned to leave. A meaty hand grabbed her upper arm, preventing her from moving away. She tried to wrench free, but the man's grip was too strong.

"Let me go!"

"No, no, no sweetie! You told me you don't have the money, but you have other things I'm interested in."

Kate swung her free hand around to slap Big T. Her hand made contact against the side of his face; the force of the slap stung her hand, but it didn't seem to dissuade the big man. In fact, it seemed to make him even more interested in her.

"Oh, you want it like that?" Big T stepped forward and slammed his body into hers. Kate sprawled back against the wall of the hallway. The smell of the man was repulsive. She detected the stink of cigarettes and booze on the man's breath. He grabbed the hand the she had slapped him with and brought it down to rest against his side. His fat rolls jiggled under her hand.

"Please, stop. I'll pay you," Kate cried out, but she could not move, the weight of the big man pressed against her.

Laughing again, Big T breathed in the smell of Kate's hair. "Too late for that, girlie. You're paying your bill another way now." He took a deep breath of her perfume. "MMmmm. I love collecting rent."

Kate tried kicking. It was no use. He had pressed himself too close for her to build any force behind her kick.

"Don't worry, Kate. You'll learn to like it. Do you know why I'm called Big T?" Big T pulled her hand down to grope his groin.

Kate fought the urge to vomit. Not wasting a moment, she grabbed him and squeezed with all her might. Big T cried out in pain and backed away, but Kate did not let go. Instead, she twisted and squeezed harder. A flash of blackness and light, followed by a loud thud, blurred her vision. Kate tasted blood in her mouth. Her jaw felt as though it were ripped off her face. Big T's cries of pain, turned to moans, somehow sounded far away.

"Stupid bitch! I'm going to kill you," Big T shouted out between groans.

Kate's vision came back, and she found herself lying on the aged carpet. It stank of mildew and dirt. Big T was holding himself, leaning against the opposite wall. *Get up and get out of here, now!* Kate stood up, her face throbbing.

"Oh no you're not!" Big T stepped toward her, his hands clenched in anger.

Kate reached into her pocket and pulled out the mace. She met her attacker face to face, spraying mace directly into the man's eyes. Big T fell back, clenching his eyes now.

"Damn you, bitch! You're dead!" He rubbed his eyes to no relief.

Kate swung her right arm around in a wide hook, burying her fist into the man's jaw. He stumbled back a step.

"Try it, asshole!"

With her left arm, she swung a hit to the other side of the big man's face. He stumbled back and fell to the floor. Unable to control her rage, she kicked between his legs as hard as she could.

"Any more threats?" she spat, blood and spit landed on the man's face.

Kate checked her pocket for her keys and turned to leave. Big T lay whimpering. He clutched his crotch, his most valued item out of commission for some time. *He won't be trying that again anytime soon.* Kate smiled and passed the onlookers that had opened their apartment doors to see what the commotion was about. Kate heard some people clapping at what she had done. The pain in her jaw was throbbing. She didn't know where she'd go, but she needed to get out of the building and back to her car. *All my stuff is up there.* The thought of leaving her belongings behind made her want to cry. Her body shook, absorbing all that had just taken place, but she kept moving.

Few people were on the streets now. Only gangs or criminals prowled this neighborhood at this hour. Kate heard footsteps approaching from behind her. Spinning around and raising the can of mace, her heart pounded. A child looked up at her, holding her hand out for change. Steam escaped the girl's mouth from the chill of the night air. She appeared to be starving. *She'd be about the same age.* Kate thought and felt a pang of guilt and sadness wash over her as she thought about the baby she had lost so many years ago. She pushed the memories away as she always did.

***

"Ma'am, are you OK?" the girl asked as she stood watching Kate stare back at her.

Kate jumped and then sighed. *I must look a wreck with my face all bruised.* Reaching into her pocket, she searched for loose change. She had none, nor did she have any money whatsoever. *I'm so screwed,* she thought as she shook her head "no" at the child. Kate turned to continue walking to her car. She was happy to see that the group of men had dispersed, leaving her car alone. As fast as she could, she unlocked the door and started the car. Her stomach rumbled and she realized she had not eaten since lunch. Not sure of where she could go, she started driving down the street. She knew she'd need a place to rest, but it wasn't safe to sleep in her car in this neighborhood. Tears began to stream down her cheeks. *What the hell am I going to do now?* She looked down at the dashboard. The low gas indicator kept flashing. She tapped it, praying it would go away. It didn't.

"Can this day get any better?" Kate hit the steering wheel. For some reason, the thought of Jared came into her mind. As hard as she thought her life was, she could not imagine what he had to be going through. Relearning how to walk and pick up the pieces as a young man from where he left off as a young teenager. She smiled, realizing how much she liked to spend time with him. She wondered if he were still up. He always listened to her and she needed someone to talk to. *I can always steal some hospital food and some ice for my face.* With that thought, Kate turned the car around to head back to her work, hoping there was enough fuel to take her there. As she drove, the memories she had repressed fought their way to the surface.

CHAPTER SIXTEEN

Kate's Past

KATE DID HER BEST to focus on the road. She reached into the glove compartment for some Tylenol to help with the throbbing pain in her jaw. Tears dripped down her face and it was making driving difficult. She slowed the car down and pulled to the side. She was tired of holding back the painful memories. Images spun before her in her mind. Most of the time she could push them down, but the little girl she met in the street had been too much, had reminded her of too much, and she couldn't fight it any longer. She squeezed the steering wheel until her knuckles popped and she began to sob.

"C'mon Kate. It's not a big deal." Derek inched his hand up her thigh. He was a handsome guy who played the drums. She loved to watch him play. Most of all, she loved the high he gave her.

Giggling, Kate pushed it away once more. "I'm only fourteen."

"It's OK with me baby. I heard you know your way around pretty good."

He pushed himself against her harder, this time pinning her hands down.

Kate gave in, it wasn't worth fighting. Plus, she was exhausted. The weed — or the booze — or whatever the heck else Derek gave her was potent stuff. She really didn't care. Anything to take her mind off her lousy life. Nobody wanted her. Living with foster parents that only used her for a paycheck. He undid the buttons of her shirt.

"No, stop," she murmured, half hearing her own voice. She batted at his hands, but it was pointless. Her muscles were exhausted, and it was all she could do to lift her hand.

"Shut up. Tease," Derek slapped her face.

It didn't hurt at all. She felt *nothing*. It was exactly what she wanted to feel. *Nothing*.

Her vision faded and her eyelids were heavy. *I just want to sleep.*

Kate slept and Derek raped her. (*No, this was long ago. I don't want to see this...*)

***

Kate woke late in the night, naked, and in bed alone. Her head throbbed. She gathered her clothes that were strewn on the floor and slowly dressed herself. *What the hell room is this?* The room stunk of body odor and trash lay in every direction. The bed was unsupported and only comprised the mattress. Used needles lay scattered. She had wound up in a drug house, no doubt. That was fine by her. Better than being beaten by her stepdad. (*No more!*)

FLASH!

***

A month later, the school nurse administered a pregnancy test — which tested positive. That was of no surprise to her. Another check to the growing list of problems in her life.

"Stupid girl! You're going to have that baby. You're going to deal with your damned mistake for the rest of your life." Her so-called dad yelled at her after hearing the news from her doctor.

Kate sat on the couch as he paced in front of her. His old pants were at least a size too big — barely clinging to his skinny frame. *Good thing he has suspenders.* She figured if he didn't, they might fall to the floor at any moment.

"What the hell am I going to tell everyone?" He turned to her, his face red and the few slicked-back hairs left on his head were standing up now.

Kate shrugged. Her head was dizzy from the pills she had taken earlier in the day.

Her stepdad shook his head. "Stupid girl." Then he proceeded to unbutton his pants and suspenders. Kate laughed. She tried to focus, but her vision was doubled.

He grabbed her face to direct her to his eyes. "I've been wanting to do this to you for a while now. I take you into my home, and you make me into laughingstock. Now you're pregnant. Now I can do whatever I want to you." (*Sick pig! You were supposed to help me! No more!*)

FLASH!

***

"Please....Help!" Kate cried. Her mouth clenched. Blood covered her mattress on the floor. She gasped for breath. *Oh my god! My baby!* She cried out again. "Please, I need help!" She prayed her stepfather would have the compassion to help her.

She lost her baby that night. (*My Baby! My poor...poor...baby! No more! Please, no more!*)

FLASH!

***

Kate focused back to her current situation. *That is not me anymore.* She wiped her face and the tears. *Not anymore.* A car drove by, the lights shining into the car. Kate looked into the mirror and saw her face, glistening wet. *Life goes on — it always does.* Kate tried to clean her face up the best she could with what she had in her car. She always wondered what her baby would have looked like, who she'd be, if she might have lived a good life.

It had taken the loss of her baby to turn her life around. Kate remembered the day she made a vow to change. She was 16 and she applied for her right to be an independent. That's when she moved out on her own. She worked many jobs to support herself while she finished up her education. She was lucky enough to get grants and scholarships. These would help her enroll in a fast-track nursing program. By helping others, the void caused by the guilt she refused to let go of was less painful.

She took a deep breath, and remembered all the people she had vowed to help. She thought of Jared. The pain and struggle he faced was incredible, yet he pushed forward. *I can, too.* She sighed and turned on the blinker. *Enough,* she reminded herself and pushed the memories back to the space she always pushed them — until another day, like she always did.

CHAPTER SEVENTEEN

Hospital Roommates

As HER CAR SPUTTERED into the parking lot of her job, Kate let out a deep breath of relief. She didn't want to abandon her car on the side of some street. It was the last possession she had. With no money, she had no idea how she could afford to pay to get her car back if it ended up towed. She would have to wait until her next paycheck before she could find any comfort. The car burped from its last gulp of gasoline remaining in the tank and stalled. She barely made it to the parking spot in time. Without any power supplying the brakes, the car rolled forward. Kate cringed as the bottom of the car scraped against a cement block. *That's one way to stop.*

The night air was damp and the sky was overcast, blocking any light from the stars and the moon. Kate wrapped her arms around herself as she walked to the building where she worked. She had always been strong and could usually seem to find a positive way to spin hard times. But tonight she could not manage to find any way to make herself feel better. She felt as though someone had kicked her in the stomach.

"What a fool! The world would be better without me," Kate thought out loud, kicking a rock into a nearby drain. A plane flew overhead and she looked up, longing for an escape. A mist formed and Kate sensed her clothes dampening. *Just where the hell am I going? Why would Jared will give a damn about how hard my life is?* Trying to push the voice in her head aside, she kept walking to her workplace. The light at the door made her feel a little better. At least inside it was warm and safe. She flashed her access card at the sensor on the door. The door clicked, the locking mechanism released. *If someone asks why I'm here, I just left something and I needed stop by to get it.*

Still wearing her scrubs, she walked past the night security guard. The guard, reading a newspaper, never glanced at her. Smiling to herself, she walked to Jared's room. Through the window in his closed door, she could see the TV was blaring a sitcom re-run.

Kate reviewed the chart on Jared's door. The nurse that had been on the night duty had never stopped to check on him. Seeing who was on duty next, Kate knew Jared would not have any other visits either. It was Becky Bronte. One of the laziest, not to mention sluttiest, nurses Kate had ever worked with at the health center. *Likely off somewhere screwing the janitor.* Kate knocked on the door. She became concerned when there was no answer. Again, she knocked and this time opened the door to announce herself.

"Jared? It's Kate. I'm coming in, OK?"

"Kate? Thank God!"

Kate closed the door behind her, hurrying in to see Jared lying on the floor. Concerned, she ran to him and knelt down to help him sit up. "Are you OK, Jared? What happened?"

"Oh, I thought the floor would be comfortable." He smiled at her. "Actually, I wanted to try walking. What happened to you?" Jared focused on her bruised jaw.

"Never mind that. You tried walking? By yourself?" Kate frowned.

"I'm tired of this Kate; lying in bed, doing nothing all the time. I want to move...on my own!"

"Jared, I understand, but you could have gotten hurt. You still need help; your muscles are still weak," Kate said. "How are your bruises feeling? Any better?"

Jared's face flushed red. "Do you have any idea how stupid I feel? I can't even change myself." He shook his head in disgust. "I'm tired of being so helpless."

"I know the feeling." Kate patted Jared on the back. "Let's get you back into bed." Wrapping her arms under his, and then with a heave, she lifted him to his feet. Jared appeared shocked at her strength. Kate laughed. "What? You think I'm a little flea?" she asked as she helped him into his bed, laying him on his back. She covered him with the blanket that had fallen to the floor.

Jared shook his head in disbelief. "Kate, you never cease to amaze me."

"Don't kid yourself, I'm not that great."

"You lifted me like a sack of potatoes!"

Kate laughed. "No, potatoes are heavier than you."

Jared looked hurt at her joke. "Am I at least cuter than a potato?"

"Slightly," Kate winked at him. "I practiced boxing while studying for nursing. Growing up the way I had to, one learns how to defend oneself. You should have seen what I did to my landlord tonight."

"Oh?" Jared looked interested in hearing her story.

Kate sighed. "He won't bother me anymore. Except now I'm homeless," she paused, "but it doesn't matter, I guess. I'll figure something out, I always do."

"Homeless? Is that why you're here so late?"

Kate nodded. "Yes, I'm sorry, Jared. I didn't know where else to go. I needed someone to talk to. You're the only person I can talk to."

Jared smiled. "It's fine, Kate. I'm glad you came. The floor was numbing my ass."

Kate laughed. "I imagine. But now I should go, since I still need to find a place for tonight."

"Kate!" Jared yelled out as she turned to leave. "You don't have to go. I'd like it if you would stay here...with me."

Kate felt a wave of relief. She didn't want to explain to anyone why she was sleeping in the break room. *But what if I get caught?* she thought. "No, I really can't, Jared. I'd lose my job if anyone found out I was staying here with you. You are my patient after all." She smiled at him.

"But, what if I fall out of bed again? I'm a horrible patient, Kate." Jared smiled back. "Plus, I can set the clock to warn us before my check-ins and you can leave or hide for that time."

Kate hesitated. *This is wrong.* She stood, weighing her options. *What else do I have?* Ashamed to admit she needed help, she tried her best to swallow her pride. "Are you sure, Jared? It would only be until I can get a new place."

Jared grinned. "As long as you need, Kate," he moved to the side of the bed to make room for her.

"Not so fast, Mr. Smooth." Her face blushed at the thought of sharing a bed with someone in her care. "I'll take the chair for now.

Jared sighed. "It's just a bed. It's not like I could make much of a move on you anyway."

"I know. It's very sweet for you to offer. I'd like to, but it takes me some time to lower my guard and let people get to know me. I'm just not ready for that. Please give me some time, Jared. I really like you." Kate walked to the chair and sat down.

"It's fine, Kate. I'm sorry I was pushing you. I like you too, and I love your company. When you're comfortable with it, you're welcome here. I'm sure the chair isn't the most comfortable place to sleep."

"Jared, I've done some things in the past that I'm not proud of. I'm not who you think I am."

"We all have our pasts to deal with. Yours doesn't bother me, whatever it is."

Letting out a deep breath, Kate closed her eyes. She tried to get comfortable, the cold faux leather chair squeaking with every move. She had lost everything she owned and did not have any idea of what she would do next. It didn't matter. She had found someone who actually cared for her and whom she cared for. Sleep overtook her.

CHAPTER EIGHTEEN

The Meeting

J-Rock's heart pounded in his chest as the car turned into a garage. *This could be the end.* His eyes searched for any chance of escape should things go awry. X wasn't paying any attention to his passenger. He was either too busy bopping his head to the beat of the song playing or hopped up on some of his product. *I could jump out and run off somewhere,* J-Rock thought. His grip on the door tightened. Instead of ripping the door open and rolling across the cement of the garage, he let go of his grasp. Taking a deep breath, he tried relaxing. As tempting as it was to run into the city, away from his past, he pushed it back in his mind. *I'm J-Rock dammit! I don't take shit from no one!* He smiled. He would meet the infamous Slice. If Slice wanted to take him out, he would not go down without a fight. J-Rock would go down in the gang history, fighting the notorious Slice. Victorious or not, J-Rock would be famous. He gritted his teeth. *Slice will not take me down.* He could feel his neck heating.

X pulled the car around to a dark spot in the garage. The light above kept flickering on and off. "They'll be here soon."

J-Rock slammed his clenched fist onto the dash. "Enough of this shit! What the hell is going on and what does Slice want?"

X jumped back at the other man's sudden outburst. "Slice don't tell me shit. Just to bring yo ass to see him."

J-Rock ripped the door's handle and kicked it open. The door nearly swung off its hinges. Swearing to himself, he stepped out of the car. He ignored the other man's orders for him to get back in the vehicle. He could hear X reach into the glove compartment, fishing around for something. J-Rock didn't care what he was reaching for, it didn't matter. Adrenaline coursed through his body. He grinned, feeling invincible. Walking around the car, he looked in the back window. J-Rock winked at the man frantically pulling out a pistol. *Good, I'll take it from him and blow his brains out.* Standing outside the driver's door now, he pulled the handle. X had locked it. The other man was pointing the gun at him through the window.

"Get back in the car!" he yelled out, the gun shaking in his hands.

"You pointing that gun at me?" J-rock asked, stepping to the side and slamming the window with his elbow. The glass shattered. J-Rock sidestepped as X fired a shot through the opening. The man didn't seem to know how to use a weapon. How he'd managed to climb the gang's ladder as he had, J-Rock had no idea. X was struggling to unbuckle his seatbelt and J-Rock used the moment to pull the gun out of his hands. He stuffed it in the back of his pants.

"Slice gonna rip your throat out!" X's belt was free now and he was trying to move to the other seat.

J-Rock reached in and grabbed him. With both hands under his armpits, he pulled the man out through the window. With a thunk, X fell to the ground. Not wasting a moment, J-Rock kicked him hard in the ribs. X grunted at the impact and struggled to crawl up to his hands and knees. J-Rock looked down on the man with disgust.

"You think you can drag me out here and pop me off?" He shook his head. "I'll kill you and I'll kill Slice. You don't know who you messin' with." He kicked X once more, sending him back to lie on the floor. X rolled to his side, huddling into a ball.

"Please," X held his hand out for J-Rock to stop. "I don't know what Slice wants."

J-Rock knelt down and lifted X's head up by the back of his hair. X cried out as J-Rock pulled. It felt good to have so much power. Reaching back, he withdrew the gun with his other hand and held it to X's head, smiling.

"No, please don't. I really don't know what he wants."

"Bullshit." J-Rock began to pull back the trigger. The sound of a car approaching stopped him from finishing the job. Instead, he slammed the man's head into the concrete, knocking him out. He noticed that X had lost his bladder, dampening his pants. *That's right. J-Rock is a man to be feared.* He hoisted the unconscious man's body off the floor. Supporting the man with one arm and his gun hanging at his side in his other hand, he watched as the BMW came to a stop in front of him. The car lights shined on the two men. *This is it.* His finger slipped over the trigger of the gun. He stood a moment, waiting to see what would happen. The waiting was getting on his nerves and he brought the gun up to the drug dealers head.

"What the hell do you want with me, Slice?" he hollered as he shook the man's body he was holding upright. "This is what happens when you piss me off."

Another moment passed. "C'mon. What? Are you chicken shit?" His anger now was flaring and he felt as though he might snap. *Keep cool.* The back door of the car opened, the sound echoing through the cold garage. A man, dressed in a black trench coat and a dark hat, stepped out of the car. He stood staring at J-Rock and the unconscious man for a moment. Then, to Jared's surprise, the man broke out into laughter, his deep voice booming. J-Rock couldn't stand the fact he was being laughed at.

"What's so funny? I'm about to blow off your dealer's head." J-Rock had the feeling he was not as in control as he thought he was.

The man walked forward, his boot heels clicking with each step. "You think I give a damn about him?" The man's voice was deep and powerful.

J-Rock felt a lump in his throat. If X wasn't important and Slice wanted him dead, he might as well pull the gun on himself and blow his own brains out. Still, he didn't let go of X. It could be a trick. "Who are you and what do you want?"

"I'm Slice. I only want to talk with you, J-Rock."

"Ok, then talk."

Slice took his hat off and stepped forward into the light. He did not look at all like what J-Rock expected him to look like up close. He had only seen him from a distance and imagined him much differently. In front of him stood an elderly man, his head completely shaved. A nasty scar ran the length of the man's cheek. Noticing the look on J-Rock's face, he smiled. "Not what you expect? I get that a lot."

J-Rock laughed. "Enough of this, you're not Slice."

In a flash, Slice flapped open his jacket. There was a whistling noise followed, by a thud and a scream. J-Rock panicked and let go of X. He expected pain, but there was none. A cry of agony brought his attention back to focus on X. He was grabbing at a knife buried in his left thigh.

"He's useless." Slice closed his jacket, hiding the assortment of knives he had strapped inside. "Shut up, X!" he shouted at the man who was crying in pain.

"OK, I'm confused." J-Rock looked puzzled. "What is going on here?"

Slice walked nearer, to stand over X and look at J-Rock. His face was creased with age and hard living. "Well, see X here, he served his purpose well, but look at him." He looked down with disgust at the man whimpering on the floor, his pants soaked. "I need someone that doesn't need a teddy bear to fall asleep at night."

X tried to stand, but fell back down, grasping the knife in his leg. "Slice, what are you doing?"

Slice ignored him and focused on J-Rock. "I've heard a lot about you. You've done a lot since the day I first met you at your initiation." He smiled, his teeth giving off an eerie glow in the flickering fluorescent lighting. "I also heard you didn't cave with that damned detective and his tricks." Pausing a moment, he wheezed as he inhaled a breath. "I want you to take over my drug operations."

X rolled to his good leg and began to crawl away. A trail of blood followed him as he dragged his injured leg across the floor.

Slice watched him a moment and turned back to J-Rock. "X sampled a bit too much of his product and has become a drain. Good at business, but bad at enforcement, and our sales are lagging. I need someone with some muscle and the ability to use it." Slice walked over and put his hand on J-Rock's shoulder. J-Rock threw it aside.

"Touch me again and you'll end up in your grave sooner than old age will do you in, Gramps." J-Rock's grip on the gun tightened. He hated to be touched. If it hadn't been Slice, he'd have blown a hole through the man's head already.

Slice laughed again and pointed at him. "See, that's what I need. So, you have an option open to you, young man. Finish X and the job is yours."

J-Rock didn't take a moment to consider the choice. People using him always infuriated him. He wanted to spill someone's blood. It might as well be X's. He hadn't liked the man from the start anyway.

X picked up his pace. The knife in his leg seemed not to matter now. J-Rock walked up next to him, kicking him over onto his back. *Like a fat beetle,* he laughed at the thought.

"Please. I have a kid." Tears streamed down X's face, his hands up, pleading.

"I don't give a rat's ass what you got." A quick flick of the trigger, blood splattered the floor and X lay motionless. At one point in life, J-Rock might have felt some remorse for killing him. Not anymore. Now he felt powerful. He closed his eyes and tipped his head back, breathing deep. A slight smile graced his face. He heard Slice clapping from behind him.

"You will be a perfect fit." Slice walked over to where J-Rock stood. J-Rock watched the blood seep from the gaping wound in the other man's head. "I'm sure you've made a few enemies along the way you'd like to dispose of. As a 'sign-on bonus,' my men can help you pay back a few debts."

J-Rock didn't need time to think. "Yeah, that dumb detective. He needs to die."

Slice didn't seem surprised at the choice. "As much as I agree, we can't touch him. It would expose me too much."

"Whatever. There are others I'd love to remove anyway. The traitor that landed me in jail, Gash. He needs to go. There's also a girl I can't get out of my mind."

Slice laughed. "Always a girl to get in the way of things. I'm sure we can find a way to get her to see how things really work."

J-Rock nodded. This was turning out to be good after all. *Can't wait to see you again, Kate.* Smiling, he and Slice walked back to the car.

CHAPTER NINETEEN

Forced Relationship

J-Rock sat on the couch across from Big T, the foulest smelling person J-Rock had ever met. The couch reeked of the fat man's odor. That, and the rotting food stuck between the cushions from his meals in front of the TV. Big T was currently ripping apart some Kentucky Fried Chicken wings. Grease covered his face and was dripping from his fingers. J-Rock felt his stomach turn at watching him devour the dead bird meat. Big T shifted in his chair and a loud rumble erupted accompanied by a loud fart. The man's stomach shook as he laughed at his bodily functions.

"Wooh! Chicken must be mixin' with the beans." Big T smiled, chicken meat showing from the gaps between his teeth. "Want some chicken?" He held out the bucket to J-Rock, the sides soaked in fat drippings.

J-Rock turned his head away. "No. I'm sick of waiting. Where is she?"

"Don't know, man. She'll be down. No way she can get in." Big T threw a bone at the trash can in the far corner of the room and missed. The bone hit the wall, leaving a grease stain, and bounced off into a dirty pile of clothes.

J-Rock couldn't stand sitting on the dirty couch and stood up. "You're wasting my time, T. I don't like wasting time." He could feel his face redden and his fists tighten. He wanted to do away with the stupid slum lord and his stench. He reminded himself of the evidence that would point the police straight to him if he followed through with taking out fat man.

Big T bit off too much chicken and began to cough, hitting his chest with his fist. Tears streamed down the fat man's cheeks and his coughs began to sound harsh. He reached for J-Rock, his eyes pleading for help as he gasped for air that would not come. J-Rock smiled. He could just let him fall to his knees and die. He wouldn't have to do anything. No one could pin a man choking on his own food on him. *Damnit. I need him for now.* Reluctantly, J-Rock pulled the man to his feet and wrapped his arms around the middle of his chest. The smell of new sweat and old sweat was almost more than he could handle. In one quick motion, he pressed against the man's middle. A piece of chicken with the bone still attached went flying out of Big T's mouth.

J-Rock let go of the other man and pushed him on the back to fall to the floor. A loud thud filled the room. Big T coughed and hacked for a minute before rolling to his side. "Thanks, bro. Stupid chicken!" He spat in disgust. "I'm going to sue their asses!"

"Shut up, T! Next time I'll let yo—"A soft knock at the door interrupted him. "OK, go get the door, you fat idiot."

Big T rolled to his back and strained to sit up. "A little help here?" He held his meaty hand out for J-Rock to lift him up to his feet. J-Rock helped him up, wiping his hands after.

"Who's there?" Big T shouted.

"Kate. My door is locked."

"Hang on, Kate." Big T nodded at J-Rock and walked to the door, unlocked it, and swung the door open.

Kate stood in the doorway, still in her scrubs. Her hair fell in blond curls, draped over her shoulders. She looked as beautiful as ever. J-Rock peered around the corner, staying out of sight.

Big T motioned for Kate to enter. "Come on in, Kate. We have some things to discuss."

"No, I'd rather not. I know I'm behind in my payments. I promise I'll pay you next week when I get my paycheck."

"Oh, don't worry about that. I do have some things to talk with you about, though. Please come in and we can chat." He smiled. "I won't bite."

"Really, I should g—"

Big T stepped out and grabbed her by the arm.

"You're gonna come inside, bitch!"

J-Rock smiled when he saw Kate swing at the big man with her free arm. T grunted at the impact, but did not let go of her other arm. In a flash, she had a can of mace out and was spraying him in his eyes. This time T let go and fell back, crying out and holding his eyes.

"You dead, woman!" T stumbled against the wall.

"You think you can just rough me up?" Kate yelled back. T received another strong punch to his face, followed by a knee to the groin. He slumped to the floor crying like a baby.

J-Rock laughed. The sight of the big man getting pummeled by the pretty girl was a riot. *Just the girl for me.* He stepped out from the shadows still laughing, but louder now. Kate looked up and it appeared that she recognized him. She stepped away from the big man on the floor.

"You're the guy from the hospital. Keep back or you'll end up like him." Kate pointed at Big T, now curled in the fetal position, holding his balls and whimpering. She held the can of mace up, pointing it at J-Rock.

"No, I won't end up like him. Nice work on that, by the way." J-Rock casually walked to the door, his hands in his pockets. "Ever since I saw your tight ass in those scrubs I haven't been able to get you out of my mind."

Kate shook her head and turned, running down the hallway. *That's the way it's going to be then?* J-Rock thought and bolted down the hallway after her. She was fast, but J-Rock was used to the streets and was faster. Just as she was at the door to the stairs, he reached around her waist and picked her up off her feet. Kate kicked and landed a powerful blow below his knees. It set him off balance a moment. The struggle just made him angry.

"Enough!" J-Rock swung her body around and threw her into the wall. She gasped and fell to the floor, leaving an indentation in the sheetrock from her shoulder. "I didn't want to have to hurt you, woman, but you left me no choice." J-Rock spat on the floor.

Kate struggled to her feet and lunged at him with all her strength. J-Rock sidestepped the punch, countering with a swing of his own. He directed his punch at her stomach, knocking the wind out of her. Kate gasped for air. J-Rock backhanded her. She fell to the floor again.

A door to one of the apartments opened and an older woman looked down at the girl on her doorstep. Kate reached up to the old lady, pleading for help. The older woman looked at J-Rock and then back to Kate. She shook her head apologetically before closing the door.

J-Rock stepped closer. "Kate, it would be better for you to learn a little faster. I have many friends and those who aren't my friends fear me." He reached down and grabbed her under her shoulders, helping her to her feet. Kate didn't resist; tears ran down her face. She looked into his eyes, ignoring the blood running from the gash in her lip. J-Rock smiled. "Why did you make me do that to you?"

Reaching into her pocket, she grabbed the can of mace she had hidden away before trying to escape. She shook her head in a way to say she was 'sorry' and stepped closer to J-Rock. In a last ditch effort, she pulled the mace out. J-Rock grabbed her arm before she could complete the motion. Yanking her hand out of her pocket, he saw the can of mace in her hand.

"Stupid bitch." J-Rock pulled the mace away and threw it against the wall.

The sound of someone approaching distracted him. It was just long enough to forget about punishing her further. Big T walked over to where they were standing. He still was rubbing his eyes, raw from the spray.

"I'm going to teach you a lesson, woman." T pushed J-Rock aside and grabbed Kate.

"Let go of her, T." J-Rock pushed T away from her.

"You saw what she did to me. No woman treats me like that!"

J-Rock pushed the man to the wall. "You don't touch her. Ever. Understand?"

Big T nodded his head that he understood.

J-Rock turned to Kate. "I'm sure this is a lot to take on, Kate," he stepped over to her and brushed hair away from her face. "If you treat me nice, I'll treat you nice."

Kate pushed his hand away.

"Kate, you're my woman now. I'm a very powerful person and you don't want to make me angry. That boss of yours made me mad. The way he treated you. Well, you won't have to deal with him anymore."

He stepped to the door by the stairs and opened it, motioning for her to leave. "I'll let you think some things over and check up on you soon — maybe over a romantic evening out." He smiled.

Kate looked confused, but didn't miss the opportunity to leave. She stepped out through the door. J-Rock closed it after she was through. *She'll come around, she has no choice.* The thought made J-Rock smile to himself. *We'll make such a nice couple!* He turned to see Big T, still rubbing his eyes. *I need to find a replacement for this fat idiot!*

Happy with how things were coming together, he made a call on his cell. A man's deep voice answered.

"Yo, Mauler, it's J-Rock. You boys done yet?"

"Done. The twink won't be botherin' you no longer."

"What about Gash?"

"Done."

J-Rock ended the call and smiled. It was great to be in power. He figured that Kate would learn of Frank's demise and link it all together. She might try to run out of the city, but he had already accounted for that. He put a couple men on task to make sure it didn't happen. She'd soon realize she had no choice but to 'love' him. He'd lavish her with gifts in return for her good behavior. Everyone could be bought.

With one of his targets gone, he could focus on the next on his list. The detective was off limits, but it didn't mean he couldn't get close to him. The security guard at the jail had pissed him off and he'd made a promise to pay him back. He'd have to do for now.

CHAPTER TWENTY

Drug Deal

IT DIDN'T TAKE LONG for Kate to come back around. The media had plastered news of her boss's death on every screen and paper in town. J-Rock was busy working out a deal with a new drug connection on some extremely potent cocaine when his cell phone rang. Apologizing to the rough looking men standing in front of him, he walked back to the car. His footsteps echoed in the large parking garage as he walked. If it were him alone, he would never turn his back on the men. Fortunately, he had an even rougher man with him for backup. Slice had assigned Mauler as J-Rock's tough man. Though Slice had told him it was only for his protection, J-Rock knew Slice was keeping tabs on him. Slice kept close track of J-Rock now, with the new power he'd bestowed upon him. It didn't bother him though; he would soon earn Slice's respect and he'd back off on the constant surveillance.

J-Rock cleared his throat, "What is it?"

"J-Rock, it's T. Your woman is here and wants to talk to you. She's a bit shaken."

"Well, send her to her room and tell her I'll be there soon. Tell her to put on something nice." J-Rock turned off the phone and walked over to the group to finish the deal.

Glancing around the group of men showcasing three briefcases full of cocaine, J-Rock nodded. An open sample of the white powder stood before him. All three men standing near were carrying semiautomatic pistols. Another man stood back with the car, an automatic rifle strapped over his shoulder. *Well, they came prepared*, J-Rock thought as he dabbed his finger into the powder and tested it against his tongue. *Another band of idiots trying to screw me over*, he thought. He nodded his approval at the lead man in the group, before turning his back to walk to the car. He nodded to Mauler. *No one gets the best of me.* J-Rock leaned against the car to watch the action unfold.

Mauler stepped close to the leader of the other gang. He towered over him by at least three feet. Even with Mauler's threatening look, the smaller man stood his ground. Mauler reached out, and grabbing him by the throat with one strong arm, lifted him clear off the ground. The other two men rushed to draw their own weapons. It was too late. Automatic fire from behind them, cut them down. With one swift motion, Mauler threw the man in his grip to the side. The man's head hit the cement floor with a heart-wrenching thud. Blood puddled under his head from the impact, his eyes stared blankly at the ceiling of the garage. The other two lay lifeless in their own blood.

J-Rock laughed, "Mauler, you da man!"

Mauler turned to face J-Rock, smiling, showcasing all the teeth he was missing. "You owe me money."

J-Rock shook his head in amazement. "I still can't believe you lifted him like that. Glad you're on my side, man!" J-Rock reached into his pocket, pulling out a roll of money, and threw it at Mauler.

Reaching down, Mauler picked up the money. He fanned it through his fingers as if he were counting it.

"Shit, Mauler! You can't count, so why fake it?"

Mauler looked back at J-Rock, scowling.

OK, I'm pissing him off now, J-Rock thought and smiled at the other man, hoping to settle him down a little bit. "Hey, I was only kidding. You need to trust me, man. I won't screw you over."

Mauler seemed to lighten up some. "A thousand dollars says I'll break the next one's neck with one hand."

That's nothing to me anymore. J-Rock nodded. "Sure, I'll go in on that." *All I need to do is find someone with a fat neck.*

A squeaky voice echoed through the garage. "Sss-so where's my m-money?"

J-Rock looked over to see the young man that was the backup. He was still holding the automatic rifle.

"You did good, kid. Hey Mauler, give the boy his money."

Mauler turned and walked over to where the boy stood shaking at the sight of the large muscle-bound man approaching him.

Mauler pulled out another wad of money and glared at the younger man. The young man held out his hand. Mauler grabbed it, yanking the arm around the boy's body. The boy, now pinned, could not reach for the gun strapped over his shoulder.

Mauler whispered into the boy's ear, "Kid, you've seen too much. I'm sorry." He wrapped his other arm around the trembling boy's head and, with a quick motion, snapped his neck.

J-Rock cringed at the sound of the bones cracking. Mauler released his hold on the body and it slumped to the ground. He stood over the body a moment before turning back to face J-Rock. *Is that a tear?* J-Rock laughed at the thought. He watched as the big man lumbered to the driver's side of the car, wiping at his eye. Noticing J-Rock watching him, he frowned.

"What?"

"Nothing."

"Dust. I have allergies."

"Uh huh."

"Really, it's dust." Mauler opened the door the car and sat down, slamming the door after him.

Dust. Mauler is sensitive! J-Rock smiled and let out a small snicker before getting into the car.

"If you're done with your, uh, allergies, I need to get back to the apartment." J-Rock grinned at Mauler. "I have a date."

***

J-Rock made a quick stop at the tailor shop before arriving at the apartment building. Now that he was near the top in the gang, many of the nearby shops didn't charge him for anything. It was a perk that J-Rock loved above all in his line of work—aside from the violence.

Mauler followed behind him as he entered the building. J-Rock turned as he entered the apartment building to face his companion. "Seriously? I'm on a date here, Mauler."

Mauler looked uncomfortable explaining himself. "Boss told me to look out for you and make sure you're safe."

"You mean Slice wants you to make sure I stay in line?" J-Rock could feel his face burning. "The old fart still doesn't trust me."

Mauler stared back at him without speaking, crossing his arms. His muscles bulged underneath the thin layer of his shirt. J-Rock knew he'd be no match against Mauler, so he dropped it. Shaking his head, J-Rock turned and walked to the elevator. Mauler followed behind him. J-Rock muttered under his breath and slammed the elevator button. He took a deep breath and turned back to Mauler.

"So will I get any privacy?" J-Rock raised his eyebrow to hint at what his intentions were.

"I brought my earplugs and my book." Mauler was expressionless.

"You read?" J-Rock asked as the doors opened.

Mauler looked at J-Rock, not saying a word.

"What book?"

Silence.

"Mauler, what book? If you don't tell me, I'll let everyone know about your crying fit back at the garage."

Mauler's face reddened. "I have allergies."

"What book?"

Mauler reached into his pocket and pulled out a Danielle Steele book. J-Rock couldn't hold in his laughter. "Romance? You read romance?"

J-Rock rolled his eyes as he stared at the big man, amazed at what a pushover he was. Mauler stepped forward and J-Rock felt the big man's hand on his chest. Falling back, J-Rock slammed against the elevator door, his breath knocked from him. His vision darkened from the impact. As his vision returned, he could see Mauler's angry face glaring down at him.

"Don't you ever tell anyone about this, kid. I don't like what I do. I do it because I have to. My little boy needs me and misses his mommy. I'm all he has and this work is all I know how to do."

The elevator beeped as it passed another floor. Mauler looked up at the numbers and then back to J-Rock; his huge forearm pressed him harder against the door. "You think I like taking orders from a young punk like you? I looked at that boy today and thought of my own kid and I pray he doesn't wind up like him."

J-Rock tried pushing the larger man away from him, but it was no use. Mauler was far bigger than him and he found himself pinned. He tried to talk, but Mauler covered his mouth.

"Shut up!" spit flew from his mouth and landed on J-Rock's forehead. "You listen. I report to Slice. Slice tells me to protect you and I will—with my life, but not for you. I do it for my kid. Slice has money set aside for my boy if I die. That doesn't mean an *accident* couldn't happen."

Swallowing hard, J-Rock looked at the man towering over him. His head was feeling light; Mauler's arm was restricting his airflow. Mauler frowned at him.

"We understand each other?" Mauler asked.

Jared nodded the best he could for "yes".

Mauler smiled just as the elevator slowed. He let go of his hold on J-Rock and J-Rock fell to the floor, gasping for air. With one powerful arm, Mauler picked him up like a bag of feathers. The elevator stopped. The doors began to open. Mauler reached out, adjusted his suit jacket, and patted him on the cheek. J-Rock swatted his hand away. The thought of killing the large man entered his mind, but he knew he'd never be able to do it. His head began to pound with the early signs of a headache.

Mauler could see the anger in his eyes. "Don't take it personally, kid. You're not the first person I've had to protect. I've had this conversation many times. There have been others whose usefulness expired and Slice had removed before you came along."

The doors were open now. Mauler turned him around and prodded him out of the elevator. *Many others? Slice will never get the opportunity. I'll kill him first,* J-Rock thought as he walked to the apartment and opened the door. Mauler was right behind him. *I'll have to find a way to dispose of this meathead too.*

As J-Rock entered the room, he saw Kate standing in the center, her face showing disgust at his entering the room. She was wearing a low-cut red dress. Her blond hair curled and hung loosely over her shoulders. She looked stunning. Unable to help himself, his eyes were immediately drawn to her cleavage. Not looking away, he stepped forward to pull her into an embrace. Kate backed away and her foot hit the leg of the small table behind her, but she kept her balance. *No, you are mine, woman,* J-Rock thought as he wrapped his arm around her waist. She hit his chest, but he pulled her closer to him and pressed his lips against hers. She resisted as he forced his tongue into her mouth. A stab of pain pulled him out of his lust as she bit down on him. Pulling back, she slapped his face and light flashed in his eyes. *She can hit, and she can hit hard,* was his thought as he fell back.

J-Rock rubbed his jaw and shook his head at Kate who was staring at him with hate in her eyes. He laughed. *What a day. First Mauler, now this slut!* She watched him as he laughed. Standing back upright, he shook his head. "You are going to learn to respect me and give me what I want. I always get what I want. The sooner you understand that, the better."

He came forward again and Kate swung her hand to slap him again, but J-Rock caught it in mid-swing. Her arm was small in his hand and she felt so delicate. He squeezed her arm; he wanted her to cry. She stared back at him, her jaw tensed. He squeezed harder and twisted. Yelping, she fell to the floor.

"Stop. Please, " she cried.

"I'll stop when I want to." He grinned down at her. "Remember who the boss is here, Kate." He raised his free hand above his head and began to swing it down when he felt a strong hand grip around his wrist. *I should have known that sap would stop me.* J-Rock turned to see Mauler shaking his head no. First letting go of Kate, and then shaking his arm free, he spat on the floor next to the girl.

"Get up, Kate. We have a dinner date. I expect you to be better behaved. You owe me respect." J-Rock turned and left the room to wait in the hall.

Gripping his hands, he turned and hit the wall in the hallway. *How dare she treat me like that? And Mauler, what the hell is his problem? They will all pay.* He could feel his face burning at the thought, then he smiled. *Kate, she'll pay tonight.* Taking a deep breath to calm himself down, he turned and peered into the room. Mauler was helping Kate to her feet. The large man leaned to her ear and whispered, "Please, do what he says and you'll survive."

Kate looked into the big man's eyes and nodded, wiping a tear away. Mauler handed her the handkerchief he had in his pocket, which she took and smiled back at him. J-Rock rolled his eyes and stepped through into the door's threshold, clapping.

"Bravo. Now let's go, Kate."

Kate handed the handkerchief back to Mauler and stepped to the doorway where J-Rock stood waiting. J-Rock grabbed her by the arm, pulling her to the elevator. Mauler walked slowly behind, keeping his distance.

CHAPTER TWENTY-ONE

Proposal

KANE WATCHED AS J-ROCK pushed a beautiful young woman into the back seat of his car. A large black man followed close behind and entered the driver's seat. Kane knew the girl from somewhere. *Is that the girl from the hospital? She didn't look happy to be with him. What does he have over her?* Kane chewed on a toothpick he had picked up from a local Chinese restaurant as he waited for the other car to drive away. Kane usually found himself oblivious to anything else but his task at hand. Such was the case when the toothpick broke and a shard of wood stuck his gum. He scowled and spit it out.

J-Rock's car pulled out onto the main street. Trying to keep a low profile, Kane followed as close behind as he dared. As traffic picked up, it became increasingly more difficult.

After an hour in heavy traffic, Kane followed the other car as it pulled into the parking lot of a small Italian restaurant. It surprised him that J-Rock wouldn't spring for something more expensive. The woman with him appeared to be a catch. Instead of pulling into the parking lot, Kane brought the car to a stop along the street. He reached for his binoculars.

J-Rock got out of the car and held the door for the young lady. She was the girl from the hospital. She wiped tears away from her face with the back of her hand. J-Rock shook his head, frustrated, and Kane watched him as he snapped at her.

What the hell was her name? Stupid old man! Kane scoffed to himself as he reached for his notepad. Kane watched as the couple entered the restaurant. While holding the binoculars, he skimmed through the notepad with his other hand. The big man who had driven the car stepped out after the couple was gone and followed behind them.

Setting the binoculars down, Kane went back to find the girl's name. *I'm too damned old for this.* He stopped at the girl's name: Kate. He opened the car door and walked to stand beside a window, looking at a menu posted on the glass. He could see inside to where the host had seated J-Rock. Kate sat next to him. He had his hand over hers. Kane watched as J-Rock explained something to his date. Kate's posture was stiff as if frozen. The big bodyguard sat at a table nearby reading a book. His drink of choice: a cappuccino; Kane couldn't help but laugh to himself.

J-Rock reached into his pocket and withdrew a small box. Kate shook her head and tried to stand. J-Rock reached over to place his hand on her shoulder and pushed her back down into her seat. With a quick swing, she slapped him across his face. J-Rock backed off and rubbed his cheek, smiling as Kate stood up again. Casually, he withdrew what appeared to be a picture and set it on the table. Kane watched as Kate sank back into her chair, shaking. They talked some more before he let her out of her chair. Kate's balance shook as she made her way to the back of the restaurant. *Probably the restrooms,* Kane thought. J-Rock stood and walked over to where the big man sat, his back to the entrance. Kane took a deep breath as he thought,

This is my chance. Better not blow it. He opened the door and walked into the restaurant.

The lighting was dim. The smell of garlic and spices filled the air. Kane felt his stomach rumble. The host took one glance at him and his choice of attire. Kane opened the flap of his coat to show his badge and with his other hand signaled the host to be quiet. A bit shaken, the other man nodded and continued organizing the menus.

Kane skirted most of the tables and customers as he made his way to the hall which, to his luck, was empty. There was one lone restroom where Kate must have gone. He walked to the door and heard the sound of a woman crying. Quietly, he knocked on the door.

"Just a minute." Kate's voice trembled and he heard a paper towel being drawn.

Kane knocked again.

More movement behind the door.

Kane knocked once more.

Finally, the lock released. Kane turned the handle. Forcing the door with his weight, he pushed himself inside the bathroom. Kate squealed, but he was too quick. Before she could let much noise escape, he had his hand over her mouth. Using his foot, he closed the door behind him.

"I'm a cop, Kate. Please don't scream. I want to help you." Kane prayed she wouldn't fight him, though he couldn't blame her if she did. After all, a cop wouldn't bust down a bathroom door on an innocent person. He felt her teeth dig into his hand. Resisting the urge to pull his hand away, he tried to calm her. "Kate, I know what he's asking of you and I know it's not what you want. I also know you feel like you don't have a choice. You must be scared for your life," he paused and she let up in her struggle. "I want to help."

He let go some of his hold around her waist and she didn't struggle. "Please. Can I let you go? This is the only way I felt I could talk to you. If you want me to go when I let go, tell me and I'll leave."

She nodded.

Kane let his hold on her go and she jumped away from him and turned to face him. Her eyes looked red from tears, and her face flushed. *She's had a hell of a rough night*, Kane observed.

"What the hell are you doing?" she asked. "You can't do that!" she pointed at the door.

Kane nodded in agreement. "I know. I'd get in serious trouble if you told anyone. It looks like you're in serious trouble yourself." He held his hand to the door. "Do you know who you're dealing with out there?"

Kate exhaled a deep sigh and fell back to sit on the toilet. She threw her hands up in disgust. "Of course I know who he is. I'm stuck. He'll kill me if I don't do what he tells me to do."

Kane frowned. "I can protect you. He's a bad man, but if you say the word, I can get you out of here."

Kate gripped both of her hands into fists. She took a breath and looked up to the ceiling, thinking. "It's not that easy. You don't understand." A tear streamed down her cheek.

"Tell me, then. Let me help you." Kane reached into his pocket and pulled out a handkerchief, handing it to her.

"There's no way to help me. He knows about my child. He's already shown he can kill anyone he wants." She wiped her tears with the handkerchief and handed it back to Kane.

"Child? Is that what he showed you?"

Kate nodded her head.

He leaned back against the door. "What else did he want?"

"He asked me to marry him." The sound of her own voice saying the words made her laugh. "The bastard asked me to marry him. When I told him no, he threatened me by explaining that he'd kill my son." Her eyes narrowed. "I'm going to kill him first."

Now this is a girl I can work with, Kane decided. "I can't let you do that, but I can lock him away for the rest of his life. I need your help to do that though."

Kate shook her head. "No, I'm going to kill him."

Kane stepped forward slowly, knowing that she was in a fragile state. He could see a heat aura surrounding her. Living all his life with his strange abilities, he had learned at a young age the different emotional auras that surround people. If he didn't handle this right, Kate would go about her own plans and never speak with him again. "If you kill him, you'll go to prison, Kate. You'll never see your child, ever."

Kate sat motionless, staring blankly back at him, lost in her own world. *Nope, that didn't work*, he admitted. Kane took another step and rested his hand on her shoulder as he knelt. She jumped a little at the contact but then focused on him.

"There are many really bad characters that follow J-Rock." Kane told her in a steady and calm voice. "If you kill him, another will rise to take his place. The cycle will continue. If you help me, we can tear down the operation."

Kate nodded. "If it doesn't work, I'll kill him."

Kane smiled. "It will work. If it doesn't, I'll help you pull the trigger." It relieved him to see that the anger showing around her had dissipated and been replaced with a calmer aura.

A knock at the door ended the conversation. "Everything all right in there? J-Rock is worried and wants an answer. Please, Kate, for your own sake, come out." Mauler's deep voice echoed through the door.

Kate brushed her hair away from her face. "Yes, I'm fine. Tell him I said – Yes."

Kane reached into his pocket and handed her his card and whispered to her. "If you ever need help, call me. I'll be in contact with you soon. We'll take him down together."

Kate, nodding, flushed the toilet. Heavy footsteps echoed down the hall, signaling that Mauler had left. Kane watched as Kate opened the door and walked down the hall. The door shut behind her. Stepping out after, he passed an old woman waiting for the bathroom who had seen Kate exit before him. He winked at her and she gasped, muttering something about people these days.

CHAPTER TWENTY-TWO

Kane's Story

"OH, DON'T BE SUCH a wimp!" Kate scowled at Jared as he did one final stretch. His legs were now much more stable, but the stretches still caused him discomfort. Jared scowled back, sticking his tongue out. Kate nudged him and he sighed before bending back down to touch his toes. The time passed quickly once he began physical therapy and was receiving regular treatment. Often, at the end of the day, he'd crash into bed after eating at 5:00 o'clock. He'd be fast asleep until morning. He glanced over at Kate, who was busy packing items of his into a nearby suitcase. Her hair glowed in the sunlight where the warm sun shone through the window. Kate sighed as she worked to pack his stuff.

"Kate, are you OK?" Jared walked forward and put his hand on her back.

"No, not really." She stopped packing and turned to face him, her eyes misty. "I'm going to miss you." Smiling, she wiped away a small tear. "I've really gotten to know you Jared — and I love that you have been a part of my life. But now you're moving on and that's it."

Jared sighed, letting out his exasperation. "Kate, I love the fact that I've gotten to know you too. It's not like I'm moving across the country. I'm going to find a job and I was hoping we could get a place together. My parents will help me get on my feet."

Kate reached out to give him a hug when footsteps echoed down the hallway. She quickly pulled away, smiling at him instead. If anyone found out that Kate had been close to one of the patients, her employment would be over and she could forget any form of recommendation.

A knock sounded and the door opened a crack. "Detective Kane. May I come in?"

"Sure, Detective," Jared replied.

Kane entered the room and nodded to Kate. "May I have a few minutes with your patient, miss?"

Kate nodded back and stepped out of the room, closing the door quietly behind her. Waiting a moment, Kane walked over to a chair asking if he could sit. Jared nodded. Letting out an exhausted sigh, Kane settled into the chair.

"She's a good catch, Mr. Stone. Don't let that one get away." Kane looked into Jared's eyes and Jared almost felt as though Kane was searching for something.

Jared felt his face redden. "I'm not sure what you mean, Detective."

"Sure, sure. Don't mind me, I tend to ramble sometimes," he said.

"Is there something I can help you with, Detective?"

Kane, still focusing on Jared's eyes, finally broke his stare. "Yes. I hope so. As I'm sure you know, I'm after the man who did this to you. I need someone to identify the suspect and stand up against him in court."

"Absolutely! I'd be more than willing to help."

"Don't jump in yet," he reached into his coat and pulled out a picture, handing it to Jared.

Jared looked at the photo and excitement rushed through him. "That's him! That's the man that was there the night I got hurt."

Kane squinted in thought and leaned forward. "That's Slice. He's a dangerous little bastard — a man known for dealing with loose ends in very harsh ways. I know, personally, what he is capable of."

Jared shrugged. "You have people that can protect me, right?"

Kane nodded. "Yes, I do. You will have protection," he paused, thinking about his next words, "but it's only right that you know what you are going up against."

"OK, so tell me," Jared said.

Kane rattled off a list of killings that he suspected Slice of orchestrating. The list included the murders of entire families, from the elders to the babies. Jared felt himself shiver.

"With my testimony, are you sure you'd have enough to bring him to justice?" Jared asked.

"Yes, I do. It won't be easy on you, though. You'll have to be careful with everything you do up until the trial and his conviction." Kane was watching Jared closely. "He's not a man who likes to be challenged."

"You said that you know personally what he is capable of. What did you mean by that?" Jared asked.

Kane shifted in his chair. "It's not something I like to think a lot about, but since I'm asking you to do something many people would run away from, I'll show you." Kane fell back into his chair and closed his eyes.

Jared sat a moment, staring at the older man, who appeared to be resting in the chair. "Detective?"

Falling back to the bed, Jared held his head as the pressure built up in his mind. It felt as though he were coming down with a massive migraine. No pain followed, but instead he felt a pull.

***

Jared's vision faded and the next moment he found himself sitting in the back seat of a car. A siren wailed. Two cops were sitting in the front of the car. *I must be losing it*, Jared thought as he rubbed his eyes, hoping it would wake him up from this strange dream. To his dismay, it didn't work.

"Kane, you have to slow down or we won't make it at all!" the cop in the passenger seat yelled.

Kane? Jared half mumbled and half thought to himself as he peered at the driver. Sure enough, it was Kane, but a much younger Kane. He wasn't wearing his normal suit coat either, but instead wore a cop's uniform. Jared inched forward and stared at the man in disbelief.

"Detective Kane?" he asked, but no one heard him. "Sir!" he said louder, but still no one acknowledged him at all. Reaching forward, his hand slipped through the protective cage in front of him. He pulled his hand back, he felt nothing. *I'm not here – but it's so real!* Jared thought and fell back to rest his back against the seat. The car made a quick turn and the tires squealed.

"Kane! Slow it down!" the other cop yelled again.

"It's my family. They are in trouble!" Kane yelled back.

"You don't know that. Shit, no one even called anything in!"

Kane shot his partner a piercing glance before focusing back on his driving, "You know about the things I see, Dave. I saw my family — they are in trouble."

"I know you see things. That's why I'm here with you, bro. But we need to make it in one piece if we're gonna do anything."

Kane slowed down slightly and took a deep breath. "You're right."

Dave shook his head. "So what is it we're going to say if you are right and we exchange some rounds? How did we know?" He laughed. "It's not like we can say you had a vision."

"I don't care. All I care is that my wife and son are safe." Kane passed a car that had pulled over to let them pass.

Jared watched the scene with disbelief. Half of him was in shock from being in what appeared to be Kane's memory and half was trying to grasp how this could be happening. The car slowed down to turn into the driveway of a ranch style home. The home was small, but well maintained. Another vehicle, which appeared to be a black Cadillac, had parked on the side of the road. The window rolled down as they passed. An older man with a gash on the side of his face smiled and waved. The car drove off as soon as the police car stopped at the house.

"Kane! That was Slice!" Dave gawked and turned to his partner. "Once again, you were right. Let's get to your family." Dave opened the door and ducked behind it. Kane did the same from his side of the car.

A woman's scream pierced the night air, followed by the wail of a child from inside the home. Another man's voice boomed. Jared could make out that he was commanding the woman to be quiet.

"I'm going in. Radio this in for me!" Kane yelled to his partner and didn't wait for a response. He made his way to the front door, his gun drawn and pointed at the ground.

Well, I can't get hurt, I guess, Jared thought, also getting out of the vehicle. He stood near Dave as the cop radioed for help. A breeze blew through the trees nearby, rustling leaves, and Jared realized he felt nothing. He smelled nothing. He could hear and see, and that was it. Ahead, Kane bashed in the door and moved inside the home. Shots rang and the sound of someone falling to the floor with a thud sent a shiver up his spine. Running to the open door, Jared peered into the room. A body lay twitching on the ground. It wasn't Kane. This body was of a smaller man dressed in a leather jacket. He still held his pistol. A growing pool of blood surrounded him. Kane was standing in the next doorway.

"This is the police. Drop your weapons and put your hands up!" Kane yelled.

A deep voice laughed. "Is that you, Officer Kane? I got a little something of yours."

"Robert! Help!" a woman screamed.

Kane took a deep breath. "It's OK, honey. You'll be OK."

"Ah, isn't that sweet? But I'm afraid it isn't so, Officer."

A window crashed. A shot fired. Kane moved and fired a shot. Jared ran after them. Another man lay sprawled on the floor, this one much larger than the dead man in the hall. Blood pooled around his body and he clutched a gaping wound in his side. He strained to lift his head before finally letting it rest on the floor. Jared watched his eyes closing and heard his last breath. Kane rushed to hold the woman who was consoling the child. Looking up to his partner who had fired from outside the window, Kane nodded in approval.

"Got your back. I'm always looking out for you. You're the psychic one; it should be the other way around." Dave said and holstered his gun. Just as he turned, a car squealed, and he yelled in surprise. "Get down! Get down!"

Kane immediately pushed the woman and child to the floor. A burst of gunfire riddled the house. Holes pierced the walls. Bits of wood and wallboard showered the room. Jared saw the other officer's back turn red as the bullets tore into his body. The car squealed its tires once again and was gone. Sirens sounded in the distance. Kane rolled off his family — they were safe. Jared moved to the open window to see Dave lying on the ground, motionless, covered in blood.

***

His vision returning, Jared sat upright. Kane still sat in the chair, his eyes closed. A tear slid down his cheek. Slowly, he opened his eyes.

Kane cleared his throat. "That's what you're up against. I lost my partner that day. He was a good friend. Help me get Slice and put him away for good."

Jared took a deep breath. "How did you —"

"It's a gift and a curse. It doesn't matter. Please, think about it, Jared. I need your help."

Kane stood up, his knees cracking, and walked to the door.

"Detective!" Jared yelled for his attention.

Kane turned and Jared nodded to him, "I'll help you."

Kane smiled back, "That's good news. An escort is outside the building to get you started in the witness protection program. And I was serious about that nurse." Kane walked out and closed the door behind him.

Jared sat in disbelief at what he had just seen. Rubbing his temples, he wondered how the detective planted those images in his mind. *Impossible. But was it? I've had plenty of strange visions myself*, he thought. He felt as though a headache was waiting just around the corner. Not present yet, but just lingering somewhere nearby. There was a light knock before Kate peeked through the door. "May I come in?"

Jared nodded. Kate closed the door behind her.

"Everything OK? You look a little pale," she said.

"Yes, I think so," he replied, his voice a little hoarse.

Kate walked to stand beside him. Jared watched her move and couldn't believe how beautiful she was. It wasn't just her physical appearance, but how much he loved being near her. *The detective is right*, he thought. When Kate was close enough, he reached out and embraced her, breathing in the wonderful perfume she always wore that he loved so much.

"Jared?" she pulled back slightly, but not giving the impression that she wanted to be out of his arms. "If anyone sees..."

"I don't care," he said and hugged her closer.

She wrapped her arms around him and hugged him back. "What happened?"

"I need to talk to you about the man who hurt me so many years ago," he said.

Kate sat down and Jared recounted all that had happened with the detective. He explained how Kane needed his help and how it could be dangerous for him. Kate listened, disbelieving at first about the vision, but she didn't interrupt him. When Jared finished, Kate sat a moment, thinking it over.

"So, what are you going to do?" she asked.

"I'm going to testify," he replied.

Kate sighed. "Good. A bastard like that needs to learn he can't get away with what he did to you and countless others." She put her hand on Jared's knee. "Just so long as you are safe."

"Kate, I —", he paused and cleared his throat, "I don't want you involved with this. I want you in my life, but I worry about you being safe."

"Don't worry about me. I've been in some bad situations and if any mean guy gives me or you a hard time, I'll rip his balls off," she said and gave him a wink.

Jared laughed and smiled back. "OK, then. I pity the thug who messes with us."

Chapter Twenty-Three

Interview

Jared sighed before stepping through the door to the cafeteria of Mike's Hardware. He'd found out about the arranged interview just that morning. The police had wanted to keep him as low-profile as possible. That meant finding him a job for him to pass the time until Slice was behind bars. A big man sat at a table and motioned for Jared to have a seat across from him. *Wow, the police went all out when finding me a job*, he thought as he took in his surroundings. The cafeteria was dirty and the walls needed painting. At least it would be a little extra income. After leaving the hospital, he'd found himself uprooted without any contact with his family or friends. The police had informed him the action was necessary to protect both Jared and those he cared for. Jared took a seat.

"Mr. Stone, I don't see any education listed on your application. Can you please explain why the section isn't complete?" The owner of Mike's Hardware looked down to where Jared sat in front of him.

A man nearby swore at the soda machine and gave it a good kick. He turned to where the two sat at a round table. "Yo, Mike, this stupid machine ate another dollar!"

The big man, Mike, rolled his eyes and turned to the other man. "Look, Fred. I'm interviewing here. Go take your break elsewhere."

"You pay squat and then you steal our money with this godforsaken soda machine!" Fred scowled and turned to walk out of the room.

Mike stood up, his belly hanging over the table. Jared caught the smell of perspiration and saw a dark spot near the man's armpits. "Fred, you see this young man sitting here?"

Fred turned to look at Jared. "Yeah, I see him."

"He's your replacement. Get the hell out of here."

"What? That pipsqueak? Right." Fred spat on the floor as he pointed at Jared.

"I'm sick of your attitude. It's time for you to leave, Fred. You can walk out or I can haul you out. You decide." Mike huffed and sat back down, breathing heavily.

He's going to keel over here, right now, Jared thought. He glanced at the other man leaving as he slammed the door behind him. Jared turned back to Mike, who still appeared to be regaining his breath.

"I always hated that guy," Mike said and looked back at the application sitting on the table.

"About my education. I—"

Mike raised his hand, "I really don't care if you got education or not. In case you didn't notice, I just got another vacancy."

Jared sighed. No one would hire him because he didn't have his GED, and this was his lowest point. Jared knew the police couldn't find anything better for him. Of all the places to work, Mike's Hardware would never be his first choice, but he needed a job.

"You know what a hammer is?" Mike asked.

Jared nodded.

"You know what a saw is?"

Jared nodded.

"You know how to count?"

Jared nodded again.

"Ok, you're hired." Mike stood up again and offered his hand, "Congrats!"

Jared stood and shook the other man's hand and cringed at how sweaty and greasy it felt. "Thank you, sir."

Mike struggled to get to his feet. "Yeah, yeah. Minimum wage with a ten cent increase annually. You start tomorrow morning. You know your way out. I've got to visit the can before I crap myself."

Shocked, Jared watched the big man hurry to the bathroom. *Oh, I hit a gold mine here for sure*, he thought and walked to the store exit. It was a job that would pay some of his bills. In reality, Kate's income paid for most of what they needed as a couple since her last increase, but it would be nice to help. It was hard enough knowing his contribution was as minuscule as it was.

The sun blinded him as he stepped outside. He glanced at his watch. If he was quick, he'd be able to catch the next bus to go home. Kate had their only vehicle and she was at work. A car across the street caught his eye as he began to walk to the bus stop. Being in a poor section of the city, a Cadillac tended to stand out. The man that was just fired from Mike's was chatting with the driver. Jared tried to focus on who it was in the car, but couldn't get a good view. He didn't want to appear obvious. The tinted windows made any effort futile.

The man talking to the driver looked up and Jared felt the man's gaze settle on him. Jared tried telling himself he was being paranoid. He focused on the ground as he picked up his pace. What if the person in the Cadillac was Slice's agent? Or worse, Slice himself? He kept moving. The bus stop wasn't much further. He'd be fine. Continuing to reassure himself, he made a quick glance back over his shoulder. The man was no longer standing by the car, but the car remained parked on the side of the road. Jared snickered to himself. *Probably just asking for directions*, he thought and chastised himself for thinking foolish thoughts.

Adjusting his tie, Jared stood with the few people waiting for the bus. The heat of the day was bearing down on him and the dress clothes he wore were too hot for the bright sun. Just wanting to be on the bus, away from the heat, he wiped away a bead of sweat on his forehead. A few moments later — it seemed like an hour — the bus pulled up to the curb. Jared gladly boarded, making his way to the back where a seat remained vacant.

The bus pulled out into the traffic. Jared glanced through the back window out of curiosity. What he saw set his nerves on edge. The car was no longer parked on the side of the road. It had followed the bus through the stoplight.

Jared tried to focus on the plate and he recorded the numbers he saw. The car was just behind the bus. He tried to see the driver, but the windshield was too tinted to make out any features.

Turning around and sinking back into his seat, Jared once again reminded himself of how paranoid he was being. A little girl in the seat in front of him peered over the top of the seat, her eyes big with curiosity. Jared smiled at her and winked. She fell back into her seat and Jared heard her whisper, "Mama, that man's weird." The mother chided her for being rude. Smiling to himself, Jared took a deep breath. *I'm overreacting, that's all.*

A few stops later, Jared stood to exit the bus and briefly glanced over his shoulder. As expected, the car was not in sight. Jared stepped off the bus. He couldn't wait to share the news with Kate about his new job.

Chapter Twenty-Four

FROM: J-Rock TO: Kane

Kane pulled his car to the side of the curb, and then stepped out into the chilly night air. He couldn't explain what it was he felt, but something was not right. After a horrible few hours of thrashing in bed, followed by waking up in a cold sweat, he had a deep concern for Mama Shayga. The street was silent aside from the occasional siren in the distance. Most normal people were fast asleep in their warm beds.

Walking along the deserted street, Kane turned into the alley where Mama made her home. A breeze drifted through the air and a piece of a brightly colored cloth flew towards him. Reaching out, he grabbed the fabric, which was charred. He picked up his pace until he saw the light of a fading fire in the distance. Arriving at the scene, he found a woman's charred body at the foot of what was once a brightly colored makeshift tent.

Kane knelt down beside the body. Mama Shayga lay in front of him, her body features barely recognizable, but it was her. He hadn't cried for a long time — the last time he had, it was over the loss of his family. Nothing hurt as much as losing a wife and child — except for this. Mama Shayga was like family to him. She was the only one who understood him. The last friend he'd had left, and now she was gone too.

Tears streamed down his face as he huddled over the body, ignoring the bits of fabric that were still on fire around him. It didn't matter. No one would see it. Mama Shayga's choice of location had always been a concern to Kane. He had tried to get her to move on many occasions, but she would not. She preferred to be out of sight from people. Memories of losing his family and his partner so many years ago surged through him. After arriving at the scene and nearly rescuing his wife and son, Slice had his gang make a last-ditch effort to hurt his family. Slice had ordered his gang to do a drive-by. Kane's wife and child had died in his arms.

Kane took a deep breath. What he must do now, he dreaded. Finding his friend murdered was horrible, but witnessing her murder would be even worse. He had to do it. He needed to know who'd done this to her — although, deep down, he already knew.

Slowly, he reached out to touch the charred remains of Mama Shayga. What remained of her skin was hot and leathery. The feeling made him want to vomit. At first, nothing came. He stayed, knelt beside her, waiting. *Why is it not working?* he asked himself, but as he did so, he began to feel time shifting. The body in front of him was no longer there and the fire did not exist. The tent was intact. Mama sat inside, smoking a pipe.

Kane ran forward and knelt before the old woman in her rickety chair. She stared past him — she did not see him. He was but a ghost. He smiled at her and reached out to touch her, but she didn't respond and he felt nothing.

"Please Mama, please. Leave now," he pleaded, knowing it was of no use.

Mama Shayga smiled at some thought she must have had. "It be fine. I be ready."

Kane jumped back, shocked. "Can you hear me?"

The old woman didn't reply and her eyes still focused on something far away that he could not see.

A car screeched to a stop in front of the alley, followed by several doors opening and then slamming shut. Men's voices echoed. Footsteps approached. Kane looked to Mama Shayga. She smiled and stood up, her bones creaking as she did. She walked outside of the tent. Kane followed her outside, standing beside her, reaching out to hold her hand. She sighed.

"Take care of dat boy. He be special. Evil and good. Watch for it." She smiled. "You be a good man. In his world, you happy."

"Do you see me?" he asked.

She stared at the men approaching — three of them, all brandishing guns. One big man was with them and the other two were much smaller. The big man stopped and pointed to the old lady, told the two men to do what they had to do. He shook his head sadly before turning and walking to the car. The two men came closer. The one with the shaved head spat on the ground. "Hey Grandma."

"I know why you here," she said and smiled. "I be an old lady and am ready."

The two men looked at each other and one shrugged. Together they ran forward; one grabbed Mama while the other punched her in the stomach. Mama gasped at the assault. Kane closed his eyes, but still kept hold of her hand. There was nothing he could do.

The man holding Mama Shayga asked his partner, "So, why are we doing this?"

"No idea. J-Rock wanted it done," the second man replied and hit her again with his other hand.

Mama coughed and blood coated her mouth. Kane wasn't sure if he could bear to witness any more of this when he saw the big man return, accompanied by J-Rock. J-Rock smiled at seeing Mama Shayga. Kane clenched his fist.

"Well, what is going on here?" he asked.

The man in front of Mama Shayga turned to look at J-Rock. "I thought you wanted us to—"

J-Rock cut him off with a wave of his hand. "Yes, and you are doing a superb job. I would like to see a little more suffering though. This old biddy is a friend of a man I hate very much."

"Sure boss. What do you want me to do?"

J-Rock turned and looked back at the big man. "What do you think, Mauler?"

Mauler shook his head, muttering. It was clear to Kane that he did not want any part of this.

J-Rock laughed. "Aw, Mauler. You're such a wimp."

Turning back to look at the man in front of Mama Shayga, J-Rock asked, "Do you like older women?"

He didn't understand what J-Rock was getting at.

"Just because she's old doesn't mean her parts don't work." J-Rock winked.

The man looked surprised. "You mean you want me to..." he paused and looked back at the old woman gasping for breath, "Oh, I, uh..."

J-Rock frowned at the man and stepped forward, getting right into his face. "What do I pay you to do? You do what I tell you to do, that is, unless you quit."

The man shook his head. "I don't want any part of this."

J-Rock nodded and pointed to the alley. "Go then. Get out of here."

Not wasting a moment, the man turned around and started walking away. J-Rock nodded to Mauler. Mauler walked after the other man and followed him until they were out of Kane's sight. Screams echoed down the alley. J-Rock turned to look at the man still holding Mama.

"You want to quit too?" he asked.

"No."

"Good." J-Rock pointed to the tent. "Take her in there and you got yourself a promotion."

The man smiled and pushed Mama into the tent. Kane turned to look at J-Rock. Pure hatred showed on J-rock's face. Kane realized what a twisted man he was. If this was the man Mama was talking about, there was no way he had an ounce of good in him.

Mama Shayga screamed and J-Rock smiled at the sound. "Good work, son. Call me when you're done."

Kane closed his eyes. He couldn't take any more of this. When he opened his eyes again, he was staring at the charred body once more. He opened his clenched hands and saw blood from where his nails had dug into his skin. He would get the bastard. He had to.

CHAPTER TWENTY-FIVE

FROM: Slice TO: Kate

WHAT IF HE ISN'T ready to be a father? Kate asked herself as she drove down the freeway on her way home from her job. She pushed the thought away. *He'd have to be ready.* The car sputtered and backfired as she tried to pick up speed to maintain the speed limit. "Shit, we can't even afford a car that works right!" she swore at herself. How could they let this happen now? The thought of taking care of a baby was both daunting and exciting. They hadn't planned on a baby — but it was happening whether they planned or not. *We'll be fine*, she smiled at the thought. One way or the other, they would be fine. This was another chance for her. Thoughts of having to give up her first child haunted her every day. Jared would be a good father. He'd do whatever it took to support the child — she knew that. Kate reminded herself of how excited she had been when the test came back positive. She hadn't been feeling well the past week, and she had noticed all the signs of early pregnancy. Not wanting to tell Jared yet, she picked up a test and tried it at work. She didn't know why she didn't want to tell Jared right away. Perhaps it was memories of her first child, or maybe she was afraid of what his reaction might be. Whatever it was, she knew now she was, in fact, pregnant. She'd tell him tonight, first thing. He needed to know, now.

She pulled the car off the freeway and shortly after that, she was parking in front of the apartment. Kate slowly made her way up the steps, thinking about how she'd tell Jared the news. She took a deep breath. *Why am I so nervous?* she asked herself. *He'll be happy!* She fiddled with the door and it swung open. Jared stood in front of her, a big grin on his face; his arms open wide for a hug. She stepped into his arms and he kissed her cheek. Smells of pasta made her stomach rumble.

She stepped out of his embrace. "What's the occasion?" she asked.

Jared smiled at her. "Guess who landed a dream job?"

"I'm guessing you!" she winked at him. "Where?"

"Oh, a very prestigious place called Mike's Hardware."

Kate laughed. "Aha! Very prestigious, indeed!"

Jared pulled her into the small kitchen, closing the door behind her. He had dressed the kitchen table with a wonderful dinner. Jared pulled out a chair for her.

"Jar—" she said, but Jared cut her off.

"I know it's not much of a job. I just can't *not* work," he said as he sat down on the opposite side of the table.

Kate listened to Jared talk about his day, all the while envisioning raising a child. She wanted to jump in and share the news, but she kept wondering how to best broach the topic. Jared finished his plate and got up to set it on the counter. He walked over and kissed her on the cheek and told her he was on his way to class. Kate looked up at him with surprise.

"Oh. I completely forgot! You have class tonight."

"Yes. Wow, don't tell me you forgot? You never forget anything," he said as he smiled at her.

"I know, I'm losing it. I just have a lot on my mind," she replied.

"I'll see you in a bit," Jared said as he kissed her on the cheek and stepped out of the apartment.

Do it! she said to herself. She couldn't understand why she was making such a big deal out of sharing the news of their baby with him. Kate picked up some plates and set them in the sink, staring down at the dirty dishes. She thought of their future life with a child and smiled, deciding to tell Jared as soon as he got through the door. He would be happy, she knew he would be.

Deciding to leave the dishes for a bit, she walked into the small living room and fell into the couch. Her feet were killing her from standing all day. Closing her eyes for a minute, she found herself drifting to sleep.

***

***

***

CRASH!

Kate jumped awake, her heart racing. Footsteps followed the loud noise. Someone was in the house. She didn't have enough time to stand or to shout. She saw a very large man standing in the opening between the small kitchen and the living room. Her mind in a panic at the stranger's intrusion, Kate jumped to her feet and stumbled back. She tried to make as much room as possible between the intruder and herself. Her throat tightened. The man looked at her, and although he looked menacing, it almost appeared to Kate as though he didn't enjoy what he was doing. He had a kind look about him, even with the large and menacing appearance he gave. He stepped closer and Kate fell back further until her back was against the wall.

"Who —" Kate tried to keep her voice steady, but it shook as she spoke, "what do you want?"

The man said nothing, but took another step. As he got closer, Kate saw he wasn't just a big man, he was a huge man. He had to keep his head down to avoid bumping it on the ceiling. A large gold chain hung around his thick neck.

"Please, take what you want. We don't have much, but just take it and leave," she said, hoping he'd listen and just leave.

Finally, the man responded as he took another step, "I can't do that, miss." He was only a few feet away now.

Kate searched around the room for anything that might serve as a weapon. Nothing was nearby except for a table lamp. She reached out and grabbed it, yanking the cord free of the wall. She realized how ridiculous it was to think she might be able to overpower such a man with a flimsy lamp.

The man gestured for her to put the lamp down, "That won't do, miss. Don't make this harder than it has to be."

He took another step and then another. He was very close now. Kate raised the lamp, ready to swing. "Why are you here? Make what harder than it has to be?" she asked, her voice a little steadier now. Sure, she would go down, but she'd at least do it fighting.

"I have to deliver a message," he said. He didn't move any further.

"You could have knocked for that," she said.

"My boss doesn't work that way," he smiled sadly.

"OK, who's your boss?" she asked, but she was afraid she knew the answer. *This is not going to be good.* Jared had bought a handgun, but it was in the kitchen drawer. She'd have to get by the man and then manage to get the gun and load it. It would never work, but it was the only way she'd be able to fight back. A lamp might give a slight bump on his head, but that was all.

"Slice needs to send a message to your man," he paused, "Jared. That's his name, right?"

Kate still holding the lamp tightened her grip. It wouldn't be much longer and she'd need to act. "How did you find us?"

He took another step — just out of reach. "No one disappears from Slice."

"Please don't hurt me," she pleaded. It was worth a try.

"You can make this easier on yourself, or you can make it very difficult. Just put the lamp down and we can make it quick."

She stood, the lamp raised above her. The cord dangled ridiculously down her shoulders, waving back and forth. Kate had barely noticed that the man had made another step closer. He was fast, and it was deceiving, given his size. She brought the lamp down with all her might. He moved to one side to avoid the attack. He was in front of her now and reaching out for her. She was quick too, and avoided his reach. His hand swung past her face and she moved away, swinging the lamp around as she did so. This time, the lamp connected squarely with the man's jaw. She heard a loud "THUMP" and saw in slow motion the glass base of the lamp shatter. The man stumbled back, holding his jaw. Blood dripped from the side of his face.

Not wasting a moment, Kate ran to the kitchen. This would be her only opportunity. She heard the big man's footsteps behind her. He was yelling to her, but she didn't know what he was saying. She focused on the drawer with the gun. Wearing only socks, her feet slipped on the linoleum. Kate tried to steady herself as she slid. Managing to keep herself upright, she slid into the cabinet. Panicking, she fumbled the drawer open. The gun lay inside. Relief surged through her, but she still needed to load it. A long kitchen knife lay beside the gun, as did a box of ammunition. She grabbed the gun and the ammunition, but in her haste, the box fell to the floor. *Shit*! she thought and moved to the next item — the knife. She grabbed it and turned to face her attacker. He was right behind her. She slashed at him with the knife. A big hand wrapped around her arm. This was it. *Almost made it.* The hand squeezed her wrist so hard it felt as though all the bones inside were crushed. She shrieked in pain. *Last resort. Scream! Scream, you stupid girl!* she thought and opened her mouth wide to yell. It was no use. The man had closed in on her and pressed his other hand around her mouth. He smelled of cologne.

Leaning into her ear, he whispered, "Please, miss. I know you are scared and I don't want to do this, but I have to. I wish I could explain, but I can't." He took a deep breath. "This is not something I enjoy doing. For your sake and your man's sake, drop the case. Move away. I can't guarantee Slice won't come for you, but you must drop the case. Next time, I will have to kill you. I don't want to do that. Do you understand?"

She nodded as a tear dripped down her cheek.

"Good, now it's time for me to leave the message. It will hurt and I'm sorry. If you scream, it will hurt more."

He took his hand away. Kate tried her best to scream as hard as she could, but the man was too fast. Blackness flashed in her eyes and a massive dull pain spread through her face. Blood dripped into her mouth. She thought he would kill her. When her vision returned, she saw he was standing in front of her. One hand grabbed her chin and held her face up. He raised his other his other huge hand and slapped her hard on the other side of the face. The counter supported her weight. Otherwise, she would be lying flat on the floor. The man backed away and balled his fist up to punch her in the stomach. Thoughts of the baby screamed through her mind.

"Baby," she whispered. "Please." She didn't know if he heard her. "Please, pregnant." She felt herself drifting out and a warm stream drift down her cheek. *Blood or am I crying?*

Through a swollen eye, she thought she could make out the man nodding. For what seemed very far away, a man's voice said, "Leave, miss."

One last hit came and it was enough to bring blackness. She was out cold now.

CHAPTER TWENTY-SIX

Bittersweet News

JARED TRIED TO FOCUS his eyes on the teacher, Mr. Foss, a large man with his jawbone buried in a layer of flab. Jared's eyelids felt as though they were weighted with bricks. *I've got to get more rest,* he thought and forced his eyes open, trying with little success of fighting his fatigue. The teacher's monotone voice didn't help.

In the middle of a speech on American history, a knock sounded at the door. Mr. Foss cleared his throat, waddling to the door to open it. Jared's chin slipped from the palm of his hand. He jerked awake and tried to listen in on the conversation that Mr. Foss was having with a man just outside the classroom. He swore he heard his name spoken. His heart raced. He had no idea what it might have been. Thoughts of Kate raced through his mind: *What if I was followed?*

Mr. Foss nodded at something and backed away from the door, letting a large police officer enter the room. Detective Kane was behind him, wearing his tweed suit coat. Kane motioned for Jared to step outside the classroom. The students all stared at him in amazement, wondering what he had done. Jared felt his cheeks color and hurried to step outside the room as the students followed him with their eyes. Kane pulled him to the side, motioning for Mr. Foss to leave them and close the door. Mr. Foss looked at Jared and scowled at him, shaking his head while muttering under his breath something about young people. His fat chin shook from side to side as he did so. Jared wondered what he thought this was regarding.

Kane waited for the door to close and then leaned forward to talk to Jared. "Kate was attacked."

Jared fell back against the wall, a lump forming in his throat. "Is she OK?" he asked, his voice shaking.

"She's at the hospital and should be OK," he paused a moment and put his hand on Jared's shoulder, "but she's pretty banged up."

Jared put his head in his hands and took a deep breath before looking back at the man in front of him. "Can you take me to her?"

"There's more—" Kane started to say, but Jared cut him off.

"Tell me on the way. I need to see her." All he could think about was seeing Kate safe. This was his fault. *I never should have agreed to testify.* Now, some jerk had hurt her. All because of him.

Kane nodded and led Jared to the exit.

***

Kane drove the car to the hospital entrance to let Jared out. The cop who followed behind parked his car behind Kane's and escorted Jared to the lobby of the hospital. Kane had told Jared on the way about the attack and how Kate had managed to call the police after the beating she had taken. The detective told him how it was a miracle she had been able to call at all given how much blood she had lost. Jared lost his calm at the news, vowing to kill anyone who ever came close to hurting her again. What the police knew at this early stage was that Slice had found out Jared's location. This was a message for Jared to stop with his plan to testify against the gang's leader.

The buzzer on the elevator signaled that it was ready to take him up to another level of the building. The cop stood next to him and didn't say a word. Jared figured it was that he didn't know what to say, and that silence was the best thing at this point. Jared stepped in and what felt like forever, rode the elevator to the floor where Kate was assigned.

Following the officer's direction, Jared paused at Kate's door. He took a deep breath before entering the room. Machines beeped from behind a curtain. Jared couldn't stand the sound of the machines working. He knew they were for Kate. Memories of his time in the hospital came back to him. *What will I do if she's hurt so bad, she goes into a coma?* But he forced the idea aside. *She'll be fine. She has to be.* He pushed the curtain aside. Kate lay in the hospital bed. Jared saw bruises covering her face, behind a ventilator feeding her oxygen. Her eyes were swollen shut and red. Whoever did this knew their work. Jared clenched his fists, his eyes pooling with tears.

Jared rushed forward and knelt by Kate's bed. He took her hand in his own and swore he'd find whoever did this, vowing to make them pay for the harm they had caused her. Trying to hold back the tears, he finally had to give in and a river and down his face.

A man walked in and Jared dried his face. It was the doctor assigned to oversee Kate's recovery. He walked to the other side of the bed and read Kate's vitals. Jared took a deep breath and stood.

"Take your time." The doctor smiled sadly at Jared.

"Will she be OK?" Jared asked.

"She's taken a lot of bruising, but that will all heal." The doctor looked at Kate and back to Jared. "Given the number of hits she received, she is doing very well. It will take some time though before she feels like herself again."

"But she'll get better? There's no permanent damage?" Jared had to make sure he heard correctly.

"Yes, she should make a good recovery."

Jared took a deep breath of relief and smiled. "Thank God!"

"Are you her partner?" he asked.

"Yes, I'm Jared Stone."

The doctor moved across the bed and held out his hand. "I'm Dr. Heath."

Jared shook the doctor's hand; his strong grip surprised Jared, given the man's tall and thin appearance.

"Kate was barely conscious when she arrived. She said that you would be here to see her and to keep you informed of her health. With all the injuries sustained, miraculously, the baby is unharmed." The doctor scanned Kate's charts.

"Baby?" Jared thought he must have heard wrong.

Dr. Heath looked surprised at Jared's confusion. "Yes, I'm sorry. You didn't know? I wouldn't have said anything, but Kate's forms show that I can share information with you regarding her condition."

Jared smiled. "How far along is she?"

"I would say around a month. Mr. Stone, I really am sorry. I wouldn't have said anything had I known you weren't aware yet," Dr. Heath said apologetically.

"No, it's OK. I understand," Jared replied. He ran his hands through his hair and took a deep breath. *Amazing*. He looked at Kate and her bruises. His jaw clenched as he ground his teeth. Not only could he have lost the love of his life, but he could have lost his son or daughter. He noticed Dr. Heath still looking at him. "I can't believe all that has happened today."

"You may want to visit the cafeteria and make yourself at home. The chair over there isn't the most comfortable, but you may be able to get some sleep. Kate has been through a lot and she's likely to sleep for a while. I'm sure she'll be happy to see your face when she wakes."

Jared thanked him and felt the rumble in his stomach. *She's OK and I'm going to be a dad!* He felt a weight lift from his shoulders knowing that Kate was OK and safe. He knew she wasn't out of this yet, but she was safe for now.

When the doctor left, Jared ran his fingers through Kate's hair while she slept. He cringed at how she'd feel when she awoke. The bruises on her face were fearsome. Leaning forward, he gave her a gentle kiss on her cheek. Again, he vowed to go after whoever had done this to her.

There was a light knock at the door, followed by Kane's gruff voice asking for permission to enter the room. Jared told him to come in. Kane walked up to stand next to Jared. He sighed when he took in the sight of Kate's bruised face and he shook his head.

"Security is outside the door. No one can get to her now. I don't know how Slice got to you, Jared. It shows how powerful he really is. It won't happen again," Kane said.

Jared lashed out, "It better not happen again! Where the hell were the police?"

"We had no reason to suspect they had found your location. Now that it's compromised, we need to find a new location for you. I know it's a lot to ask," Kane replied. "Jared, I'm really sorry this happened. I let you down."

"Tell me what you are going to do different this time so that it won't happen again." Jared shot an angry glance at the detective.

"We'll get you to a different location. You will have twenty-four-hour protection. At any point in the day, the police will be available should any danger befall either of you," Kane replied

Jared nodded. "If it happens again, I'm sure it won't be just a *message*. It better not happen again."

Kane agreed and patted Jared's shoulder. "Not much longer and this will be all over. Slice will be past history."

Jared watched the man leave, wondering if the detective believed it himself. Turning back to look at Kate, he decided the first thing he would do would be to ask Kate to marry him. They would get through this together.

Chapter Twenty-Seven

Awakenings

THE SOUND OF THUNDER snapped Jared away from his dreams. Unable to sleep, he turned to look at this wife, sleeping soundly beside him, her blond hair draped over the pillow where she lay.

After a long hospital stay, Kate had made a good recovery. As soon as she was able, Kane had relocated them, warning Jared to lie low until he obtained enough evidence to bring Slice to justice. Once they were set up in their new apartment, Jared had called a Justice of the Peace and he and Kate eloped. Kate was now far along in her pregnancy. Jared thought about how happy Kate and their soon-to-be-born baby made him.

They had already run the tests for gender and been informed that they were having a girl. They'd already picked a name: Lila. Kane decided it would be best if Jared did not find a job, given the result of his prior attempt to work.

Reaching his arm around Kate, he pulled her close. A bright bolt of lightning flashed and thunder cracked. *I won't be getting much sleep tonight,* he thought. He was a light sleeper and any noise kept him awake. Still, he closed his eyes to try to get at least a few hours of sleep.

As soon as he began to drift off, thunder boomed outside. Kate sat up, her eyes slowly opening.

"Shhh...it's just a storm. It's OK." Jared rubbed her back and she slipped back down to sleep, mumbling something about dishes. Jared smiled to himself, wondering if Kate was stuck in an endless cycle of washing dishes in her dreams.

Resigning himself to being unable sleep, Jared rolled out of bed. *Maybe a few minutes of getting up will help me settle down again.* He decided to walk to the baby's room. They had just finished it.

Scuffling to the baby's room, Jared rubbed his eyes that didn't want to stay open. *Just one full night of sleep. Is that too much to ask?* he asked himself as he opened the door to the baby's room.

***

Lightning lit the room and Jared blinked at the brightness, raising his hand to cover his eyes. What he saw stunned him. It was as though he were seeing through the room into another room. A man's shadow stood in the light standing over another shadow on the floor. The shadow moved and turned to face him. More lightning flashed and Jared saw himself, but his head was shaved and was holding a gun. The shape on the floor was that of an older man, blood pooled near him. It seemed the man holding a gun saw him too because he looked surprised. The man shook his head and began to raise the gun to point at Jared.

Thunder clapped and the light faded from the room, as did whatever it was Jared had seen. His heart pounded. He walked back to bed, his legs shaking. No sleep came to him.

His mind kept focusing on the shadow he saw. *What is happening to me? I must be tired, that's all.* He tried to reassure himself that it was nothing, but it had been too real.

CHAPTER TWENTY-EIGHT

Protected Witness

HAVING SPENT THE REST of the night half-awake, staring at the shadows on the walls, Jared could barely function the next morning. Embarrassed to tell Kate about what he had experienced the night before, he tried his best to fake being sick. He tried acting like he had a horrible headache, but he knew Kate wasn't buying it. She had a way of seeing through things like that. For some reason, though, she let it go.

Spending the morning resting and getting some much needed sleep, Jared woke to the sound of the buzzer to the door. He heard Detective Kane's voice over the intercom. Kate pressed the button to let Kane enter the building.

Great. I wonder what he wants, Jared thought to himself as he got dressed. His head felt light and he knew he could use another hour or two of sleep. Kate opened the door to let in the detective.

"Hello," Kate said.

"Good afternoon, Mrs. Stone. I have some updates on your husband's case. Is he available to talk with me for a few minutes?" he paused a minute. "Oh, this is a friend of mine. She has helped me with a lot of my cases in the past."

"Jared isn't feeling his best today, but I'll see if he is up to talking," Kate replied and walked to the stairs.

"I'm up. I'm up," Jared yelled down as he walked down the stairs.

Kate shook her head that she didn't know what Kane wanted as Jared walked by her. Kane stood in the doorway, still wearing his trench coat. A woman stood behind him, almost hiding behind him, hunched over. Her hair was a ragged and gray. She wore layers of clothing, all worn well beyond presentable. Kane smiled at Jared, his craggy face looking as friendly as it possibly could.

Kane stepped forward and shook Jared's hand. Jared helped the detective with his jacket. The woman behind him backed away and crouched lower as Jared stepped forward. Seeing the woman shy away from him, Jared stepped back. Kane noticed his reaction and turned to the woman, whispering something in her ear. He turned back to Jared.

"Jared, this is an old friend of mine, Ms. Shayga. She is very smart with a lot of things and I have asked her for help from time to time."

He stepped away from the woman and she glanced at Jared, shifting her eyes from him to the floor repeatedly. Jared felt as though each time the woman looked at him, she was looking at something else besides him. Her focus was not on him, but more like *around* him.

Jared tried to look away from the woman and slipped his hands in his pockets. He offered the detective and his assistant a seat at the small dining table in the corner of the room. Kate mentioned she would make coffee for everyone. Kane took a seat, but the woman preferred to stand near the door, unmoving, watching him.

Strange woman, Jared thought and tried to focus his mind on something else as he sat down next to the detective. "So what is this all about, Detective?"

Kane shifted in his chair, smiled at Jared. "We've gathered more evidence on Slice and I think with your testimony, we have a good enough case to prosecute him. Are you ready to testify?"

Jared felt his stomach turn inside out. Slice was a notorious criminal and was responsible for countless murders. His concern was not for himself, but for Kate and the baby. *But what about all the people that could die if I don't?* he thought and exhaled a deep breath. Kane watched him, his brow wrinkled.

"I'll take care of you and your family, Jared. They won't get to you." Kane put a reassuring hand on Jared's shoulder. Jared could see a mustard stain on Kane's sleeve. *He can't eat a hot dog without getting mustard all over him and he's my protection?* Jared laughed to himself at the thought. He knew deep down that the detective was a good man and not someone to mess with. He also wanted the gang leader to pay for hurting so many people.

"I'm scared," Jared told him. "You must make sure we have protection. If I sense my family is in any danger, you can forget it."

"It will all be fine. I swear it," Kane smiled and patted Jared's shoulder. "Let's cook this bastard."

The woman Kane had brought with him limped forward and walked to a wall where a small mirror hung. She peered at it oddly. Jared only saw the woman's reflection looking back at her, but the woman appeared to see more. Her multicolored rags hung off her like bright flags. She turned to look at him sitting at the table with Kane and then back to the mirror, muttering something under her breath. She turned back and limped to where Jared sat and leaned forward; her breath smelled of decay.

"Different lives you live." She reached out to grab his cheek and Jared pulled away before she could touch him.

Kane stood up and pulled Ms. Shayga back. "That's enough, Mama. Let's go get some lunch." He pushed the woman forward toward the door as he walked behind her, one hand on each of her arms. Her face lost its color; Jared wasn't sure, but it appeared to him that her eyes had turned a grayish white. Kane turned to shrug at Jared.

"Ms. Shayga is a little *eccentric* sometimes. We'll show ourselves out." He opened the door, ignoring the woman's incoherent babble. "I'll be in touch, Jared." He nudged the woman through the door and closed it after they had exited the apartment.

Jared stood up and walked to the door, pressing his ear against it. He listened to the muffled voices.

"That boy, he in danger. He be the one." The woman's voice was trembling.

"The one? You mean the one that is different?" Kane asked.

"Yes! The one. The other one be evil! This one in trouble!" Jared heard her tapping the door with her finger.

Footsteps walked away from the door and down the stairs. Jared jumped when he heard Kate as she walked over and held a cup of coffee in front of him.

"Jared? You all right?" Kate sounded concerned.

Jared, realizing how stupid he must look, smiled. "Yes, I'm fine."

"So what was that all about? Something about Slice? And who was that woman?" Kate frowned.

Jared explained the meeting with her, avoiding anything about the strange woman. Kate had the same reaction as he did. "Jared, we have to think about the baby. It's not just you and me anymore.

"I know. But I'm the only witness that can identify him." He reached out and pulled Kate closer into a hug. "I have to do it. This man needs to be locked up. Kane is going to make sure we're fine."

Kate shook her head in frustration. "He'd better."

Jared smiled at her and Kate rested her head on his shoulder. Jared peered around her at the mirror on the wall. *What on earth had that woman seen?* he thought, and caught himself imagining a pair of eyes staring back at him, ever so faint.

Chapter Twenty-Nine

Revolution

J-Rock sat in his car, prepping himself for what he came to do. *He has to die. He's old and I do everything now anyway.* He took a deep breath. Slice had taken him in and taught him how to be a man. If Slice hadn't helped him when he did, he'd still be stuck as a pathetic shit of a boy. *Slice wouldn't hesitate to kill me, and I'm getting too powerful for him. If I don't do it now, he'll kill me first!* J-Rock rubbed his eyes. Lack of sleep was getting to him. Ridding himself of Slice had been weighing on him for some time. He glanced at his watch. It was almost time to follow through with the plan.

Screw Slice. He has to go. His chest fluttered, thinking about it. He was going to finish it. A storm was forming in the night sky.

J-Rock stepped out of his sports car, slammed the door shut, and walked to the entrance where a guard stood watch. J-Rock nodded to the guard, who opened the door for him. Behind it was a grand lobby with a spiral staircase climbing high to the next floor. Marble floors graced the room.

Slice's bodyguard, Ryan Crill, stood in the center of the room. A man of medium build, but not one to mess with if one could help it.

Ryan had been a Navy Seal in a prior life. He wore a crisp suit and J-Rock could see the outline of a gun holstered behind his jacket.

"We ready to finish this?" J-Rock asked.

"Slice is in his study. He's not feeling his best today." Ryan motioned toward the study. "We need real leadership and we're counting on you to provide that."

J-Rock nodded and walked to the study, his steps echoing through the mansion. He stopped at a large wooden door and knocked.

"It's about damned time you came back with my tea," answered a hoarse voice followed by a cough.

J-Rock opened the door and stepped inside the study. Slice sat in a large leather chair wrapped in a blanket. He jerked his head back in surprise at seeing J-Rock.

"What's the meaning of this?" Slice began wheezing and fought to catch his breath before coughing.

J-Rock pushed up his sleeves and stepped closer. "Why do you ask? You already know why I'm here, Slice."

The storm outside was getting stronger and a wind-driven rain pelted the glass in a nearby window.

Slice laughed. "Stupid boy. I have a cold and you think you can do away with me?" he cleared his throat and yelled, "Ryan!"

Ryan opened the door and stood beside J-Rock, his hands held down in front of him, "Yes, sir!"

Slice motioned to J-Rock, "Take care of this trash for me. It seems my pupil has outgrown his usefulness."

Ryan didn't move.

"Ryan! Do as you're told!" Slice's eyes bulged at his order.

"It's over, Slice. You have grown weak." J-Rock took another step closer. His heart was beating faster. *This is going to be difficult. Why is this difficult?* He had killed countless people but an old man was going to be the hardest of all. He felt a tear forming in his eye. How was that possible? J-Rock pushed his emotions aside.

Slice threw his blanket off and stood. His body had become more frail than J-Rock expected. It was not a cold. Slice was ill. It was time for him to die, and he should go like a man, not a weak, sick dog. *There, that's better.* J-Rock smiled to himself.

"Help!" Slice yelled out.

J-Rock reached to behind his back and withdrew his Glock.

Footsteps rushed to the room. J-Rock didn't take his focus off Slice. He was old and sick, but he was still deadly. He raised the gun to the man's head and smiled.

"I'm doing you a favor, old man."

"No, you can't do this. I made you."

"We had a good run." J-Rock aimed at his head.

J-Rock sensed Ryan taking a defensive position behind the door as the footsteps came closer.

Slice knelt to the floor, his hands held up, pleading. "Please, I'm afraid to die. What will become of me?"

"Aw, c'mon. That's just pathetic." J-Rock shook his head.

One moment, Slice was cowering, and the next he sent a long silver knife flying at J-Rock.

J-Rock sidestepped and narrowly avoided being stuck with the knife. He pulled the trigger and the job was done. A chunk of Slice's head separated and his body fell to the floor. J-Rock reached down and grabbed Slice's journal from the table next to the chair.

The lightning storm outside the mansion intensified and knocked out the power. Another bolt lit the room and blinded J-Rock. He shielded his eyes and turned. For a moment saw himself in another room. *Impossible.* He began to raise the gun but then the vision was gone.

Gunfire took his attention away from the old man's body and what he thought he had seen, and he took a defensive position on the other side of the door. Ryan exchanged fire with the other guards.

"I thought you said you took care of everything?" J-Rock yelled over the gunfire.

"Half the guard is on my side. This is the other half."

J-Rock counted four guards positioned in the lobby. They were pinned in the room.

"So where's your half? Did they plan on attending this party?"

Ryan grinned at J-Rock, his eyes wild. He obviously loved the action. He reached into his pocket and pulled out a flash-bang. "3, 2, 1..." Ryan threw the flash-bang into the lobby.

J-Rock turned away before it detonated. Automatic fire echoed through the mansion. Ryan motioned for J-Rock to exit the room.

"Time to go!" Ryan stepped through the door, firing rounds.

J-Rock followed after, staying low and sticking close to Ryan.

Ryan's contingency had the high ground and fired down from the balcony.

Gunfire whistled in all directions as Ryan led J-Rock to the door.

"What about you?" J-Rock asked as Ryan motioned him to a parked pickup.

"I'll clean this up. You need to get out of here to jump start this revolution."

J-Rock nodded and clapped Ryan on the back.

As he drove away, he heard a loud explosion and in the rearview mirror saw the mansion engulfed in flames. *Holy god. I could have been in that.*

That was the last time he saw Ryan.

CHAPTER THIRTY

Power Shift

KATE SHIFTED IN HER chair as J-Rock told her the news; she hated the feel of leather. Nothing he told her was unexpected. J-Rock had spent much of his time away from her, on business trips. During the times he had been home, he'd lock himself in his study, along with his *closest* friends. He never included Mauler in his trips and always told him to keep watch of her while he was away, since a rival gang had taken an interest in bringing down J-Rock. Kate had no problem with Mauler; in fact, they'd become friends. Whenever J-Rock would get in one of his rages, Mauler would give her the private nod they shared for her to be on her *best* behavior, as in, do whatever J-Rock says and don't question him. Kate had learned early on that J-Rock was unstable. Often, he'd have sampled his own product, amplifying his chronic paranoia issues. He was sure people were watching him at all times. What people, Kate did not know. Whenever Kate questioned him, she'd pay a steep price. Kate rubbed her belly. She was close now to delivering their first baby together, and she worried about how he'd treat his own child.

"Slice is no more. I'm in charge now." J-Rock smiled, his face twitching. He clutched a journal in his left hand. Kate noticed that it had blood smeared on the cover. His eyes darted to Mauler, who stepped forward. J-Rock jumped to his feet. He withdrew a Glock from inside his sports coat, pointing it at Mauler.

"Stay there, Mauler, or I'll kill you too." The big man stepped back against the wall, staring back at J-Rock. Kate thought she could see the vein in Mauler's muscled neck pulsing.

"The only reason I haven't done away with you yet is because my wife likes you. You have a choice, Mauler. Work for me or die." J-Rock winked at Kate as she sat still, afraid to make the situation any worse. "It's not that hard a choice, really. What's it going to be?"

Mauler nodded. "I will work for you."

"Good. I didn't want to make an orphan of your firstborn son." J-Rock sat back down and hid the gun back inside his jacket and then laughed. "Well, I take that back. I don't really give a shit." He looked back to Kate before opening a small tube and pouring white powder on the table.

Kate took a deep breath, exhaling silently and slowly as not to show J-Rock her disapproval of his habit. She watched as he bent forward and snorted the powder. He leaned back into the couch.

"I've got some other things to settle. This day has proved to be a busy one and I have a few loose ends to take care of." J-Rock stood up and shook his head, pinching at his nose. "Damn, that's good stuff!" He looked down at Kate still sitting; she felt as though he had almost forgotten she was there. "Tonight will be a special night. You're going to show me how happy you are." He smiled and walked to the door before turning to Mauler. "Do anything stupid and both you and your son will pay for it."

Kate watched as he left the room and waited a few minutes before standing up and turning to Mauler. Her heart sank at how worried he looked. She walked over and hugged him. "I understand what you're going through." She looked up to him, his eyes glistened with tears.

"I know you do, Kate." Mauler smiled down at her, hugging her back, his giant arms wrapping around her in a bear hug.

Kate pulled away and nodded at him. "Do you remember when J-Rock," she paused and rolled her eyes, "*proposed* to me?"

Mauler nodded his head.

"I wasn't alone in the bathroom."

Mauler frowned. "What do you mean?"

"A man walked in to talk to me. A detective."

Mauler was expressionless. "Kate, I don't like where this is going."

"Hear me out. I trust you, Mauler, and we are both in a bad situation here."

Mauler nodded his head in agreement and crossed his arms. "Go on."

"He wanted to help me. I was hoping that Slice would get tired of J-Rock at some point and things would work out on their own. Now, that isn't going to happen." Kate wiped a small tear away from the corner of her eye. "We need his help."

Mauler exhaled a deep breath. "Kate, if J-Rock ever finds out, it's over for both of us. He'd kill us right now if he knew we were even talking about this."

Kate smiled. "You think I don't know that? This has to end. I'd rather be dead than live the rest of my life as his little servant."

"What are we going to do?" Mauler's voice sounded flat and determined.

Gotcha! Kate smiled inside. All this time Mauler had seemed to be unwavering in his dedication to Slice. Now that his son's life was in danger and Slice was not around to protect him, things had changed. Mauler had become a friend to her, but she would never have shared the information about the detective until now. "Let's go shopping. I need to get something nice for the *celebration* tonight with my husband. We can set up a meeting at the mall."

Mauler sighed. "Let's do some shopping, then." Reaching into his pocket, he withdrew his keys and motioned toward the door.

***

Kate took a deep breath as she sat at a table in a corner of the food court at the mall. Her eyes darted from face to face as people passed by her. Mauler had not wanted to talk with the detective, but stood off some distance keeping watch over her. Kate looked down to the full plate of Chinese food she had bought and grimaced at the sight of it. Food was the last thing on her mind as she anxiously waited for the detective. She hadn't bought it because she was hungry, but thought it might take away suspicions from any passersby. *Where are you? I want to get this over with*, she said to herself as she picked up a fork and moved food around on her plate. Looking at her watch, she sighed.

"This is stupid," she muttered to herself and had started to stand when she saw a man in a brown trench coat walking over to her table. She noticed he had a coffee in his hand and had already spilled it on his shirt. He also had a newspaper. She sank back into her chair. As he came closer Kate recognized the detective.

Kane pulled out a chair at the table next to Kate's and sat down, glancing only briefly at her. Kate's pulse beat faster in her neck. She took a deep breath and picked up her cell phone as if she was talking into it. "I'm sorry, I'm really scared right now. It's risky meeting you."

Kane began reading the newspaper and spoke in a hushed tone, "I know you are. It's the right thing to do. J-Rock is a powerful, dangerous man and needs to be brought in before he hurts any more people."

Unable to hide her feelings, Kate shook her head. "I don't care. I need to make sure both my son and my baby are safe. It's come to a point that they'll be safer now if I help turn J-Rock in. He's losing it. He was bad before, but it's getting worse." She sighed and smoothed her pants, trying to relax, but it didn't help. "You have no idea what it's like to be with him." She wiped away a tear as it streamed down her cheek.

Kane scanned the people seated and walking around them before turning the page on the paper. "I know he's a bad man. You should have called me sooner." He paused and took a sip of his coffee. "It doesn't matter. Work with me now. Help me get some evidence on this guy and I'll get him put away."

Kate nodded, the phone still at her ear, wiping her eyes with the back of her hand. "He's lost it. Sometimes he is almost a different person." She paused as a child ran by. "One minute, he's the bastard that I've always known he was and then a moment later, his whole attitude changes. His look changes. I can see it in his eyes. They almost shift to show compassion." She laughed. "I've never told anyone this. It must sound crazy."

Kane frowned. "No, Kate, I don't think you're crazy. A lot of people think I'm crazy because I see things they don't. I've noticed something different about J-Rock. He's not like everyone else. There's more to J-Rock than we know. I think there is more to him than even he knows. He's probably as confused by what is happening to him as we are."

Kate rolled her eyes. *What the hell am I getting myself into? This guy's a nutcase,* Kate thought as she glanced over to the man sitting at the table next to hers. *But he's all you have — and he's right. Something is different about J-Rock.*

"So, what are we going to do, Kate? Are we a team?" Kane set the paper on the table and turned in his seat to face Kate. "Is that brute with you?" he nodded to where Mauler sat at a table reading his book.

"How? How did you know?" Kate's eyes were wide with surprise and she almost dropped the phone before placing it on the table.

"I told you, Kate, I see things others don't. He's a good man who's made bad decisions in his life and is stuck. A friend of his told me Mauler's story. Ask him about Daryl sometime." Kane took another sip of coffee, spilling some on the table. "Stupid oaf," he said to himself as he wiped the spill with a napkin.

Kate shook her head in confusion. "Daryl? What ar— it doesn't matter. What do you need from me?"

Kane smiled at her. "J-Rock is going through a transition of power. Slice has been eliminated and J-Rock is now in control. He's been sending a lot of information out to his followers and much of it electronically. He's been using his cell phone a lot, which has fewer restrictions for the authorities to tap into." Kane beamed, proud of himself. "It was recorded that a huge shipment of cocaine came into port yesterday." Kane leaned back in his chair. "He mentioned something about a log book that Slice maintained. It contains all the contacts and shipping records of prior shipments. It also lists shipments scheduled up to the point of Slice's death. J-Rock is the owner of that book now."

"I saw a book he had with him today. I don't know how I could get it away from him." A pang of hopelessness creeped in.

Kane nodded. "I know. It would be difficult, I understand. If you can get that book away even for a moment, call me. I have been watching J-Rock without much of a break, hoping to catch him slip up somewhere. So far, he's been very careful, but if I can get that book, we can lock him away for good."

Kate stood up and adjusted her pants over her pregnant belly. "I'll do what I can. If there's no other option, I'll find a way to kill the bastard myself." She motioned to Mauler and they left the detective still sitting at the table.

When they were outside, Mauler turned to Kate. "How did it go?

Kate shook her head, frustrated. "Pointless. I need to get the book J-Rock has with him all the time." She looked back at Mauler, noting the concern in his eyes. "What are we going to do?"

Mauler shrugged. "What we have to do. Get the book."

Kate nodded her head in agreement. "Right. Get the book."

CHAPTER THIRTY-ONE

Time Line Switch

J-ROCK PULLED THE CAR to a stop near the ocean wall and rolled the windows down to let the cool air flow through the car. He took a deep breath, exhaling slowly. The air was heavy, laden with salt and the strong smell of fresh seaweed. His heart rate slowed down from the fast beat it had been racing at before he stopped the car. *This is getting to be too much. This work is going to kill me,* he sighed at the thought. *Slice needed to be removed. He would have killed me soon enough. I was getting too powerful for him,* J-Rock nodded, trying to convince himself. He reached into his glove compartment and removed the journal he'd taken from Slice's lifeless hands the same day he had shot him point blank in the face with a pistol. Blood spatters covered the front of the journal. He ran his fingers over the dried splotches before opening the journal.

Inside were the details of Slice's contacts and various transactions. J-Rock flipped through the pages and a photo slipped out and landed in his lap. He reached down to pick it up and jerked his head back at what he saw. The photo was of J-Rock and Kate at their wedding, right before taking vows. He scowled at how frightened Kate looked. *Fool. She hates me.* He sat the photo down on the seat next to him. He stared at the photo, ignoring the sounds of the ocean. *She's afraid of me. That's the only reason she's with me. Why can't she see? I love her...I would never hurt her! Unless, of course, it was for her own good.* An image of him hitting her the night before flashed in his mind and he laughed. *Well, she deserved that one. She brought it on herself.*

A seagull cried in the distance and he moved to set the picture down when he noticed something in it he hadn't noticed before. A man in the background, beyond the wedding group, across the field, stood watching. The man's shape seemed familiar to J-Rock, but he couldn't remember where he had seen him. The image wasn't that clear, so the figure was hard to make out. Then the realization hit him. It was the detective who had harassed him when he finished his time in prison. But how did he know about the wedding? And why?

"Kate, you bitch. What are you up to?" His hands tightened into fists and the photo crumpled in his hand. *Time for another chat.* He looked at the clock, 10:59.

Motion caught his eye in the rearview mirror and he glanced up to see an unmarked car come to a stop some distance away. J-Rock cursed under his breath about cops when his vision began to waver. He put his head between his hands as he tried to focus, but it was no use, he was slipping. To where, he did not know.

***

After what felt like an hour, but in reality was only a matter of minutes, his vision came back and he was staring at the clock. It wasn't the car clock, but a clock on a microwave. *What the hell?* J-Rock looked around the strange room. He was in a kitchen, much smaller than his own. A familiar voice called to him.

"Honey, can you please get me some water?" Kate asked.

J-Rock walked to where the voice was. In a small living room, Kate sat on the floor, doing some sort of stretch. He stared at her in disbelief.

"What is going on here?" his voice wavered.

"What do you mean?" Kate looked back at him, confusion on her face.

J-Rock pointed back to the kitchen. "I was just — I was sitting," he paused and rubbed his eyes, muttering to himself. "It's got to be the drugs." He began to laugh and Kate frowned.

"Drugs? Honey, what are you talking about?" She shook her head, confused.

J-Rock ground his teeth. He hated being caught off guard like this. "Kate, you did this. You want to kill me. You've always wanted to kill me." His voice grew louder, "What have you done, Kate?"

"What on earth are you talking about, Jared?" Kate stood. "Have you lost it?"

J-Rock could feel his rage reaching its limit. He stepped forward in a burst of anger. Kate tried to step back, but he reached out and caught her hair, yanking her close to him as she yelped in pain. He held her head close to his face and leaned forward to whisper in her ear.

"Don't you *ever* talk to me that way. You live because I let you live." He spat on her face. His body felt light. Regaining control is always good. He wrapped her hair in his hand to pull a little harder and felt some give way. Kate cried with pain.

"Jared, what are you doing? Please, let go!" Kate tried to pull away, but she could not move.

Jared. No one calls me Jared. "Stop calling me that!" J-Rock let go of her hair and pushed her back.

Kate tripped on a toy and fell backward onto the sofa behind her as she cradled her large belly. She looked up at J-Rock standing over her; the color on her face had disappeared. J-Rock didn't wait a moment before stepping closer, his hand raised in the air to slap her across her face. He began to swing. Before his hand made contact, he found himself outside of his car, walking and yelling something about Kate.

J-Rock turned and could see other people watching him. Detective Kane was not hiding in the shadows, but was out of his car, watching him, curiously. J-Rock looked down at his clenched fist, opening it slowly. He had ripped hair from Kate's head, but there was nothing in his hands.

CHAPTER THIRTY-TWO

Observation

A STINGING SENSATION CREPT up Jared's arm as his vision slowly returned. He staggered from lightheadedness and his heart raced as he tried to regain control of his surroundings. A picture of him with Kate caught his attention and he felt a wave of relief at the realization that he was back in his apartment. Kate sat on the couch, her hand holding her cheek; there was blood running down her chin from a gash in her lip.

Did I hit her? I couldn't have. No, it's not possible. What is happening to me? Jared swallowed as he rubbed his forehead, confused.

"What the hell is wrong with you?" Kate was back on her feet, her face flushed with anger. She stepped forward, shaking her fist at him. "If you ever hit me again, I'll chop your balls off! You could have hurt our baby!"

I did hit her. Jared stepped back a step. He had never seen Kate this angry. He raised his hands up apologetically, "Kate, I don't know what's going on here. Plea—"

"Please what? You hit me! We were talking about your job and then you just snapped. I'm leaving for a while."

Jared felt a flood of shame spread through him as he reached out to hug Kate. She batted his arms away. "Kate, please. I don't know what happened. Please. Believe me. I would never hurt you or our baby."

Kate shook her head. "You just *did*. You hit me." Her eyes were watering now. Seeing Kate hurt, knowing he was the cause of her pain, was more than he could bear. "I'm going out and I might be back, I might not. I don't know what I'm going to do right now." She walked around him, leaving some distance between them to avoid any form of contact.

Jared let her go, sinking to the floor as he heard Kate slam the door behind her. "What is happening to me?" he muttered as he tried to recollect the events. *First, I was talking to Kate, and then I was somewhere else. There was a nice car and I was at the beach.* The thought made him laugh. "I need help." *Where was I? I was somewhere else! I didn't hit Kate. I would never hit Kate.* He sighed and then remembered seeing a familiar face when he was walking around in confusion. "Kane! Kane was there." The thought that someone familiar was there who might have witnessed the event brought some relief to him, but deep down he knew if he were wrong he'd be admitted to an asylum. *But what do I have to lose? My wife thinks I'm nuts already.*

Jared got to his feet and took a deep breath. Kane wouldn't report him if he thought he were crazy. He was too important to his case. Jared walked to the kitchen to find Kane's business card on the refrigerator. Glancing over to the microwave clock, the time shown made him pause a minute — a few minutes after 11:00. *That's about the same time I felt strange last time*, he thought as he retrieved the business card and picked up the phone. Taking a deep breath, Jared dialed the number.

"Detective Kane," Kane's voice greeted him.

"This is Jared Stone. Can we talk?"

"Jared. Is everything alright?"

"Hell no! It's really strange and I need someone to talk to about it. I was hoping you might have a few minutes." Jared rolled his eyes at himself. *There's no way he's going to believe any of this.*

"I like strange. Hit me."

Relieved, Jared continued. "Bear with me. I have had strange visions."

"Visions? OK. I know there's something unusual going on with you. I can see it in your aura. Is it just visions?"

Aura? And I was worried he'd think I was nuts, Jared laughed to himself. "What do you mean by aura?"

Traffic sounded in the background and Kane tried to speak over it, "Everyone has an aura around them, negative or positive. Yours is different and I've seen it change — as if you are trading your body with someone or *something* else."

"Trading my body? How is that possible?" Jared's voice shook as a chill crept through his spine.

"Yes, almost as if you are shifting in and out from time to time. Did something happen?"

Jared felt his heart beat faster, "Yes."

"It's going to get worse, Jared." Kane's voice was flat.

"I hit my wife. I would never hurt her. What is happening?" A tear streamed down his cheek at the sound of his own voice admitting to hitting her. "I don't know what to do. I would never hit her. She saved my life. I'm scared."

"I don't think it was *you*, Jared. Somehow you crossed paths with another realm." He paused. "Ok, I know how that sounds. But this other spirit that you are mixing with is an evil Jared. We need to find a way to eliminate its path to you."

Jared scoffed. "Ho—"

Kane interrupted, "I'm still working out how. Do you know if this happens at any certain time of day?"

Hesitating a moment, Jared responded, "11:00 or so. I think it's usually around that time of day."

"Yes, that makes sense."

"It makes sense?" Jared laughed.

"Yes. Try to keep yourself in a safe place around that time each day — away from people you love, Jared."

"This is crazy. I don't know if Kate's coming back anyway. This time, I really screwed up. I've never seen her so angry with me."

"We'll figure this out. You remember the woman that was with me when we stopped by the other day?" Kane asked.

How could I forget? Jared thought before saying, "Yes, I remember."

"I'm going to bring her by as soon as possible, around 11:00. She's a bit strange, but she sees things others do not. She might be able to offer some assistance. Is that OK with you?"

Jared sighed. "I've got nothing else to try. Sure."

***

A day had passed and it amazed Jared at how silent the apartment was without Kate. He had spent most of the last twenty-four hours in a depressed state, thinking about what to do about getting Kate to forgive him. He stood in the kitchen staring at his reflection in the mirror. *What happened? Why did I hit her?* He kicked the floorboard in frustration as he tried to think back. Throwing his hands up in frustration, he exhaled. "I'm so god-damned confused!"

The buzzer made him jump and he glanced at the clock. 10:30. *It must be the detective.* Before buzzing his visitors in, he took another deep breath and tried to collect his thoughts. "Here goes nothing," he told himself before he clicking the button to let Detective Kane into the building.

Jared opened the door when he heard the knock. Kane stood in the hallway, disheveled as ever. Behind him, the older woman, still dressed in brightly colored rags, peered from around Kane's back. When she saw Jared look at her, she ducked behind the man like a little child would. *Oh, I can see this is going to be good,* Jared laughed to himself as he motioned the two to enter the apartment.

Kane walked in as the old woman clung to his jacket, doing her best to avoid Jared's gaze. Once inside, Jared closed the door and tried not to laugh as Kane tried unsuccessfully to remove the woman's grip on the back of his coat.

"It's fine. Let go!" Kane gently brushed Mama Shayga's arm.

Mama Shayga shook her head and pointed at Jared. "He not right. No, no. He be the one, he be." Her hand shook. Jared could see her knuckles were swollen from arthritis. "I go home. Dis no place to be. Dangerous."

"No, he needs our help and you owe me." Kane yanked his jacket free and pulled a chair out from the table. Before the woman could react, he moved her into the chair and then seated himself in the chair next to her. Kane motioned to the clock. "So, you say 11:00, this weird thing happens?"

Jared nodded. The smell of Mama Shayga was starting to get to him. *God, when was the last time she showered?* He felt his nose wrinkling as he tried to ignore the smell of musty, old clothes. "Yes, I think so. I'm not even sure when it happens. Everything sort of blends together. Sometimes it's really quick. Others, well," he paused, "well, this last time I was violent to my wife and I hit her."

Kane didn't say anything. Jared almost felt as though the detective was staring into his soul. Jared stood still a moment and his head felt a little light. *What the hell is he looking at?* He felt awkward with the man staring at him.

"Do you feel anything right now?" Kane asked, still staring.

"Well, no," Jared lied.

"Are you sure? You need to pay attention to what you're feeling. The more you know about this, the more you might be able to control it." Kane frowned at him, staring at something, but not at him.

"Oh. I don't like this. It be happening. The worlds are too close." Mama Shayga covered her eyes and rubbed them with the palms of her hands. When she removed them, her eyes had lost their normal color, replaced by a dull gray shade as she focused on Jared. "Yes. It's happening now. You see his aura, Kane? He's shifting."

Mama's correct speaking surprised Jared. He squinted as he tried to keep focus as his vision blurred. "What? What aura? What the he—" he stammered, his knees buckling. Something tugged at him, rushed through him, almost as though his insides were shifting. The small room faded and the next moment he was in a large and beautifully decorated room. Kate stood in front of him, holding her face, tears streaming down her cheeks. *No, not again.* The large room faded, replaced by his familiar surroundings, and Kane was seated in front of him again. Mama Shayga was standing now, her hand on his shoulder as she peered into his eyes. Jared still sensed the pull and he tried desperately not to get drawn into the current. "Please, help me." He heard his voice tremble from some faraway place.

"Focus, Jared. Focus on what you are feeling. Maybe we can find something that triggers the transfer." Kane stood up and walked over to stand next to Mama Shayga, his face tight.

The pull was increasing in strength. Jared felt himself slipping again. Grasping at anything, he concentrated on the apartment and his real surroundings. The pull became increasingly stronger. Pain exploded in his mind. It was the worst migraine he had ever had. Screaming in pain, Jared sensed himself falling to the floor. Before the impact, his vision faded. This time he could not fight it.

CHAPTER THIRTY-THREE

Ghost

J-Rock held onto to his head, trying to block the pain. The last few moments were the strongest feeling he had ever experienced. The pulling sensation was as if his soul were being plucked from his body. This was followed by being pushed back and finally waking up on a strange floor in a room he had never seen. He moaned; his head throbbed and he rolled onto his back. A woman gasped. He tried to focus on the sound, but his vision was unsteady. The only thing he could make out was a mixture of bright colors and an overpowering odor.

"He's completely transferred. This one is evil," a woman's voice pierced his mind as J-Rock tried to cope with his headache.

"I see it too. What can we do?" a man's familiar voice replied.

"Wait is all."

J-Rock heard himself moan as he tried to sit. The room's overhead light was blinding and his vision slowly became clearer. He squinted from the light. A man stood in front of him, looking down. The stained trench coat gave him away.

"Kane!" J-Rock clamored to his feet. Pressure in his head nearly sent him falling back to the ground, but he fought to regain balance.

The man put his hand on his shoulder to help steady him and J-Rock batted it away.

"Just take it easy," Kane cautioned.

"I should have known you were part of this." J-Rock backed away from the man and focused on the woman next to him. Fear flooded his mind as he realized he was looking at a ghost. "You!"

Mama Shayga backed away a step. "Yes, I know you too." Her voice shook. She turned to Kane and raised a finger pointing at J-Rock. "That is an evil man. Evil. He's a murderer."

"You are dead. You can't be alive. No. It's impossible." J-Rock reached behind him, searching for his gun, but it wasn't there. He scanned the room for something to attack with. Anything. The only thing he saw of any use was the chair he was leaning on for support. In one quick motion, he grabbed the chair with both hands and threw it at Kane. Kane blocked the object with his arms. The chair crashed to the floor. Kane reached for his weapon. J-Rock lunged before Kane could draw the gun from its holster. He tackled the older man to the floor. *Now I'll kill you once and for all,* J-Rock heard himself laughing. He had wanted this for so long. Kane tried to use his weight to get into a better position, but was no match for him. J-Rock rolled himself on top while driving his fist into Kane's face.

Mama Shayga howled and leaped onto his back. Pain surged through him as she dug her nails into his cheeks, tearing skin as she pulled back. His body tensed and he elbowed the woman, sending her to the floor gasping for breath. "You're next, bitch." J-Rock yelled to her.

Kane didn't waste any time, trying once more to recover and gain an advantage. Using his weight, he tried to throw J-Rock off of him. It gave him enough motion to free a hand and swing at the younger man's face. J-Rock blocked the hit, partially, but it was enough for Kane to roll free.

If he gets that gun out, it's over. J-Rock started to stand when he noticed a weight used for a doorstop and picked it up. Kane had his gun drawn now, but J-Rock had the advantage of speed and swung with all his might. Kane couldn't move aside in time and the weight made contact. A sickening thud sounded. J-Rock relished the noise. Kane collapsed to the floor. His energy spent, J-Rock rolled to his back, panting from the exertion of the struggle. His head spun. He continued to contemplate how he had gotten into this mess. Watching the ceiling fan spin above him, he laughed. It surprised him and scared him, hearing the sound of his voice cackling. *I'm a madman. This is it. I've lost it...officially lost it.* The thought made him laugh even louder. Rolling his head over to the side, he saw Mama Shayga balled up in the corner, her bright clothing in a heap wrapped around her. She was fighting to recover from the hit he had given her. She pulled herself to her knees, coughing.

J-Rock rolled to his side. "What do you think you're doing old lady? We aren't done yet."

Mama Shayga fell back and sat down, pushing herself with her legs to the wall next to the door. She raised her hands up to hide her face as if she thought that if she couldn't see him, he couldn't see her. She whispered incoherently into her arms.

J-Rock spat next to where he lay and grimaced at the blood. He touched his lip, scowling at the pain. *That old man packs a punch,* he thought as he got to his feet. Kane lay unconscious at his feet, blood pooling under his body from the blow he had taken to his head. J-Rock ground his teeth. *The old fool almost got me!* he thought and kicked Kane with a force strong enough to break the man's rib. Kane's body absorbed the kick, but a moan escaped his lips. His gun had fallen to the floor and lay next to him. Confident Kane would give him no more trouble, J-Rock reached down, picked up the gun, and checked to make sure it was loaded.

His gaze fell back to the old lady huddled against the wall, still muttering under her breath behind her arms. She shook as though she were shivering.

"Oh, shut up already, woman!" J-Rock shouted, pointing the gun at her as he stood over her, glaring. She saw him aiming the gun at her and began to sob.

"Please! Leave us be. This not your world." She shook her head at him, pleading with her eyes.

"I had you killed...or at least I was told you were killed." He scratched his head, the gun pointed to the ceiling. "Well, Mauler and his goons will have to answer to that I guess." He rolled his eyes, pointing the gun at the woman's head, the tip of the gun pushing into her skull.

Her sobs were stronger now. She dipped her head down to get as far away from the tip of the gun as she could. "You don't understand. You're in a different world. The life you know is not the life you have here." She pointed to a picture on the wall.

J-Rock glanced over at the photo, frowning at what he saw. It was a wedding photo, and Kate was happy to be marrying him. Her smile was the happiest smile he had ever seen her wear.

"What the hell is going on here? Who's playing this game with me?" His face flooded with heat. Turning back to the woman, he shouted, "Answer me!" She yelped as he grabbed her by the hair and yanked her to her feet, pushing her back to the wall.

A tear streamed down her cheek. "Please, leave things be here. Don't ruin it for your other life. Let them be happy." She nodded to the photo. "Two worlds," she croaked as his other hand tightened around her neck. He released her at the sound of approaching footsteps. The door swung open. To his surprise, Kate stood in the doorway. She stood motionless, her mouth open at what she was seeing.

Smiling, he winked at her and held out his arms for a hug. "Hi, honey."

Kate backed away, but J-Rock reached out, pulling her close, the gun planted against her back. He dragged her into the apartment, closing the door behind them. He pushed her to the floor. "Wow! Quite the party we have here."

Looking around the room, Kate locked eyes with Mama Shayga. The older woman shook her head as if to tell her, "Don't try anything, this one is crazy." Kate looked back to J-Rock standing over them, the gun in his hand. She cleared her throat. "Jared? What are you doing?"

"Don't call me that!" J-Rock rushed forward and stared down at her. "Never call me that!" Spit flew from his mouth, showering her face. He backed away and laughed, shaking his head. "This crazy woman is telling me I'm not who I am and that I'm in some other world." He paced the room. "The thing is — she's already dead. So either I'm crazy or she's telling the truth." He stopped and looked at the two women sitting on the floor in front of him. "So, I'll just have to kill you," he pointed the gun at Mama Shayga. "Just for the heck of it, and then kill him — because I've always wanted to." He pointed the gun at the detective, still unconscious. He glanced back at Kate, "If the old biddy is right, well then your lovely Jared will answer for it when he's back. Though hopefully we can spend some quality time together before I go."

Kate lunged at him. J-Rock swung his hand at her, catching her in the face with the side of the gun. She grunted and fell to the floor, holding her cheek. Blood poured through her fingers. "What have you become? You're a monster." She wept. Mama Shayga crawled next to her, comforting her. "Kate. It's not Jared."

"Kate, your man needs to give you some discipline. What kind of wimp am I in this world of yours?" He spat in her hair and pointed the gun at Mama Shayga once again.

The old woman looked into his eyes. Where before there was fear, now there was hatred. "You are a pathetic being. Kill me, but know that you are nothing."

J-Rock laughed. "Nothing? The gun I'm holding says differently." He cocked the gun with his thumb. Mama Shayga closed her eyes. Before he could pull the trigger, a weight hit his calves and he lost his balance. He felt himself falling backward. Reactively, he pulled the trigger hoping to still hit the woman, but it was too late. The bullet landed in the table slightly above her head. J-Rock felt the air from his chest forced out as he hit the floor. He panicked, still unaware of how he had fallen. He tried to swing to his side to stand, but his shoulder was pinned and a rush of pain surged from his arm. "Kane!" he half thought and said aloud at the same time.

Kane was now on top of him, using his weight to keep him pinned. The older man smiled, blood dripping down the side of his face. "Yes. You need to finish your own jobs, son. I may be old, but I love putting little shits like you in your place."

J-Rock felt the man pulling the gun free from his grip. Kane raised a clenched fist up in the air. "Now it's time for me to return the favor. Nighty-night." His fist came down and J-Rock saw a bright flash of light followed by blackness.

CHAPTER THIRTY-FOUR

Evidence Hunt

JARED SNAPPED AWAKE TO a horrible pain in his head. He forced himself to open his eyes, ignoring the bolt of pain as his eyes took in the light of the room.

"Kate, he's awake," a big voice whispered, followed by rustling of papers and a drawer slamming shut.

Footsteps rushed over to him. He could smell the sweet aroma of Kate's perfume. She placed her hand on his back to help him sit.

"God, my head feels like I was hit by a truck." Jared rubbed his temples and squinted at Kate hovering above him. Her face showed worry, but it was odd, it didn't seem genuine. "Kate, where am I? Am I me or the other me?"

"Honey, just relax. You fainted and hit your head," Kate replied and motioned to someone across the room. "Mauler, go get a cold compress for J-Rock".

J-Rock. So that answers my question, Jared thought. He jumped to sit up and look around the room. Kate put her hand on his chest, telling him to relax. His head hurt and needed to lie down, so he laid back. "Kate, look, I'm not who you think I am."

"I know you're not. That's why I'm helping you. If you weren't who I thought you were, I'd hit you over the head to get peace a little longer." Kate rubbed his back with her hand until the other man returned with a cool rag. She laid it across his forehead.

Jared jerked back at the shock of the cool cloth, but relaxed, realizing how good it felt. It surprised him to find his vision was clearing. Kate knelt beside him. He saw her face had fresh bruises. Mauler stood in front of them, casting an uneasy look at him sprawled on the floor. Jared thought about how good it would be to drift off and just sleep. At least here, Kate didn't hate him — well, maybe the guy he looked like, but not him. *No, I need to figure this out. I can sleep later. Who knows what the hell the other guy is doing in my world?* Jared shook his head at the thought and freed himself from Kate's clutch. Kate fell back, frowning. She had a look as though she was afraid he might have switched already.

Jared smiled. "It's still me. But we need to talk," he said as he got to his feet. The pain in his head had lessened. He almost felt normal.

Kate, with real concern now, watched him stand and then stood up. "Yes. I need your help."

"OK, maybe we both need the same things. What is it, Kate?"

Kate folded her arms. "I've been in contact with a detective and he may know of a way to take care of my problems here. I need to protect our baby and my son."

Jared raised an eyebrow. "A detective? What kind of stuff am I into in this world of yours?"

"Well, let's just say you are now the leader of a notorious gang involved in drug trafficking, murders, and any other crimes you can think of," Kate paused and cleared her throat, "so you need to be stopped."

Jared nodded. "Yes, I'd say I do need to be stopped. But how?"

Kate stepped forward. "The detective I mentioned, Detective Kane, he m—"

"Detective Kane?" Jared cut her off. "I know Kane."

Kate grimaced. "This detective, he mentioned a log book that J-Rock keeps of different illegal activities. If we could get that book, we could get him locked away."

Jared nodded. "OK, so where is it? Let's go get it."

"Well, that's the problem. We aren't sure where it is."

Jared made a deep sigh. "Why is nothing ever easy?"

Kate nodded her agreement, crossed her arms, and paced the room. Jared watched her and thought about how eerie it was to see the woman he married in a much different situation. She looked tired and battered but still beautiful. Kate stopped pacing, looking over to Jared and biting her lip.

"How long do you have here?" she asked.

Jared shrugged and shook his head. "I have no idea, and I don't even know what triggers this other than a time of day. The longest it's lasted is about an hour."

"Well, we need you here until we find that book. There isn't much time left. He's really getting worse." Kate frowned, glancing to Mauler, who stood in the same spot nodding his head in agreement.

Jared walked over to Kate, reaching out to rest his hand on her back. He pulled away from her when she stepped away, fear in her eyes. "I— I'm sorry. I didn't mean to frighten you."

"No, I'm sorry. When J-Rock touches me, it's either to hit me or, well, he's rough."

Instead of moving further away, she turned to face him. She stepped forward and shook her head in disbelief. "What is it like in your world? Why are you so different — yet everything else is the same? I look at you and I see my bastard husband, but you look *nice*." She reached up and touched his cheek. "J-Rock got this scar from a bar fight. You don't have that where you are from, do you?"

Jared shook his head. He wanted to kiss her. *She's not Kate. Well, she is, but she's not. This is messed up!* he thought, and this time, he was the one that stepped back. "This is too much. My head hurts."

"I know the feeling. This is a lot to grasp. We need to search the house for that book and we need to start now. Mauler, you check his study," she pointed to a closed, ornate door. "J-Rock — I mean Jared, just look around with me and tell me if you start to sense anything funny. We need as much time as possible."

"I will do what I can, Kate. I really don't have any control over this." Jared frowned. "Plus, I need to make sure you — I mean the other you — and my baby are safe."

Kate's face flushed. "Dammit! I need you here right now and I will do everything I must to keep you here. You don't understand! J-Rock will kill me if he discovers anything about me going behind his back." She sighed, throwing her hands up in frustration. "We're wasting time."

Jared walked to the couch, scanning the room. *If I were J-Rock — which, technically, I am — where would I hide a journal?* he thought and began rummaging around through all the drawers he could find, but it turned up nothing.

They searched most of the house with no one having any luck. It amazed Jared, the wealth J-Rock had accumulated. *Crime does pay*, he was thinking when a bolt of pain stunned him where he stood. He dropped to his knees. Cradling his head in his hands, he cried out. His vision began to fade to a dark tunnel. Kate's voice echoed in his ears.

"No! No! Not yet! Please, Jared. Don't leave! We're not ready...fight it. Please! Fight it."

Jared looked toward the wall as a circle began to peel away. He was staring into another room. It was the kitchen of his apartment. He could see himself, lying on the floor, but it wasn't him, it was J-Rock. Blood surrounded his body and his hands were tied.

"Jared! Please..."

The pain was pulsing in his mind. It was almost as if someone were splitting his head in two with a knife. Concentrating on Kate's voice, he tried to block the pull toward his own world. They had stopped J-Rock somehow. Jared's felt his body falling back, but instead of landing on a hard surface, he sank into something soft.

"Jared...don't go. Please don't go. I need..."

The blackness began to subside. A soft light from a nearby night-light broke through as he opened his eyes. Kate hovered above him, her eyes glistening with tears. *But which Kate is it?* he thought, then saw the big man standing nearby, worry etched on his face.

"Wow...that was a headache," Jared said as he wiped sweat away from his forehead.

Kate lunged forward, wrapping her arms around him. Her body shook as she cried, "Thank God!"

It felt good to have Kate — even though it wasn't his Kate — hug him. Her pregnant belly against him reminded him of his own Kate. He wondered what it would take to get his Kate to ever forgive him. Maybe someday she'd believe him that he wasn't nuts and that there was another world.

Once Kate let up crying and pulled herself back upright, Jared smiled. "OK, let's find that damned book."

CHAPTER THIRTY-FIVE

Sports car

THE NEXT HOUR WAS spent brainstorming where J-Rock might have stowed the journal. They searched the entire house with no luck. Jared, feeling his stomach rumble, realized he hadn't eaten all day. His body was beginning to feel shaky. He turned to Kate, who looked as exhausted as he did.

"I need to eat something. I won't be able to deal with another headache if I don't. You look like you need a break too, Kate." Jared smiled at her, trying to lighten the mood, and he put his hand in his pocket. His hand brushed against something. He pulled it out. It was a key, but he had no idea to what.

Kate saw him hold the key out and pointed, "That probably unlocks the journal, but it's no use until we find the damned thing."

He put it back into his pocket and scavenged his other pockets. He just now realized he was wearing different clothing than he remembered putting on in the morning. No other items were in his pockets that might offer any help.

"What are we going to do? We're screwed." She shook her head in frustration. "I guess it's meant to be."

Mauler, who still was standing — Jared thought he must never sit down and hardly ever spoke — actually spoke for once. "Well, we could call Kane. If J-Rock comes back, well, I'm sick of the scumbag. I'll just kill him and be done with it."

Mauler's tone sounded surprisingly kind compared to the man's ominous look and size.

Kate smiled back at Mauler, "No, you won't. Your son needs you." She sat back, her pregnant body sinking into the cushion of the couch. "But we can call Kane. He might give us some idea of what to do. I really thought we'd find the journal."

Kate stood up and walked to the phone to dial Kane's number. As Jared watched her, a thought crept into his mind. When he had switched some time back, J-Rock had been driving a sports car. They hadn't searched that yet. He glanced over to Mauler.

"Which way is the garage?"

The big man led him through several rooms and into a hallway leading to the garage. The door opened. Several cars lined the parking pads. A sleek red Ferrari 458 Spider sat on one side of the garage, gleaming. A Hummer H3 sat parked next to the Ferrari. Crossing his fingers, he walked over to the sports car and sat in the driver's seat. The car was immaculate. It made him wonder what dealing trips this particular car had been on. Reaching over, he opened the glove compartment. Inside lay a thick, clasped book, locked shut. Jared felt his heart hammering in his chest. *This is it*, he thought as he reached for the book. Slipping his hand into his pocket, he pulled out the key and unlocked the book.

Smiling, Jared held the journal up to show Mauler. "This guy is done. I'm going to jail soon!" Jared laughed.

Mauler took the journal and scanned a few pages. The man's face lit up as he grinned. "Let's get this to Kate!"

Half running, Mauler and Jared entered the room waving the journal in the air. Kate, still on the phone, saw the book and laughed. "Kane, get over here. We have the book."

Jared looked at Kate and thought how radiant she looked. She looked incredible when she smiled. Kate saw him watching her and blushed. She walked to him and embraced him. "Jared, thank you."

"I'm happy to help you, but I really need some food, now." Just holding her, he could feel his arms shaking.

Kate nodded and looked concerned for him. "Jared, hang on. You've lost color in your cheeks. Please, just a little longer. We need you to hang on until Kane can get the book."

Nodding, Jared moved back and fell into a chair. He could hear voices faintly in the distance.

A man's voice, "It's been too long."

A woman's voice, "He be fighting it."

And yet another woman's voice, "Jared, honey, come back"

Jared raised a hand to his forehead, which had started sweating. The pain had crept back into his mind. *Kane! Get over here!* he thought as he rested his head against the cushion.

The pain came in waves and subsided as he fought to stay with Kate and Mauler. From time to time, he'd hear them talking to him, trying to get him to focus. After what seemed to be hours, Jared heard a man's voice, one that matched a voice from his own world. *Kane...thank God!* The blackness crept back on him when he heard Kate's voice, but which one? His Kate or J-Rock's Kate?

A woman cried, "Jared...don't go!"

Another woman cried with a similar voice, "Jared, I'm sorry."

An older woman coached, "Don't be fighting it...Come back"

The room melted around him, then reformed as he fought the pull a little longer. The room melted once more. He could not fight any longer. His head hurt. He was exhausted. Slowly, another room formed around him. It was his kitchen. He was home. Kate hovered over him, a welt on her face from a hit she had taken. He was safe at home, and Kate, in another world, was on her own.

CHAPTER THIRTY-SIX

Plans of Mice and Men

KATE WATCHED AS HER husband began to stir from bed. Jared had slept the remainder of the day and through the night, well into the next afternoon. She rubbed her eyes, trying to fight off the dryness. Reaching over, she wiped Jared's brow with a damp towel and checked for signs of the fever he had been fighting. She sighed in relief when she saw him open his eyes and smile at her.

"Kate, you're here! Please don't be mad at me." He winced, half expecting her to get angry.

She smiled back. "No. I'm not mad," she paused and glanced back to the half-open door of the bedroom leading into the living room. "Detective Kane explained everything. It still doesn't make a lot of sense to me, but it explains this," she pointed to the welt on the side of her face.

Jared frowned, "Oh my God, Kate. Did I do that?"

Kate nodded and continued, "Jared, I really don't know why this is happening. Kane said something about another world or timeline.

That woman, she's really strange." She nodded back to the door and whispered, "They are out there waiting to make sure you're OK. They wouldn't leave, so they have been sleeping in the living room."

"How long have I been out?" he asked, frowning.

"You've been out awhile. The first time you came back was this afternoon. You would wake and scream, holding your head, then fall back under." A tear ran under her eye and she wiped it away. "Jared, you scared me so badly! What would I do without you?"

Unable to contain it, Kate began to sob. Jared reached out and wrapped his arms around her. She could feel her jaw tense and felt the urge to pull away. *It's Jared*, she reminded herself and fell into his embrace.

After a moment, she looked up into his eyes, "I — we — need you. I don't know what you are going through. Whatever this is, I hope you aren't losing it. Tell me what you need me to do so I can help you get through this and we can have our Jared back?"

Jared looked into her eyes, "I wish I could tell you. I don't know what can be done. I think this is something I have to do alone." He gave her a squeeze.

"No, you never have to go it alone. We are here for you, Jared." She looked at his worn face. *This is killing you*, she thought, her throat tight. "What is this other world like?"

Jared let go of her. "Kate, whatever happens, if I switch again, you need to run. Do what you have to do to stay safe."

"Jared, you're scaring me. What do you mean?"

"It's a long story. I think Kane should hear it too."

***

Kate half-listened to Jared talk to the detective and the strange woman. The idea of another *her* in another world was too much to handle. *This can't be happening,* she laughed to herself. But it was. Her husband, by most accounts, was off his rocker. There were two strange people in her living room feeding into his paranoia: a detective prone to clumsiness and a strangely dressed woman who appeared to live on the streets. To top it all off, she was expected to believe it all — and she *did*.

"Kate, you and your baby could be in danger." The detective's gruff voice made her jump. "If what Jared says is true about him helping the *other* you in providing evidence and another switch happens, J-Rock may retaliate by hurting you or the baby."

The thought of the baby getting hurt made her heart race. "What do we do?"

Kane shook his head. "We don't know. It appears that one of them, Jared or J-Rock, needs to die to stop the switch from happening." He focused on Jared. "We need to make sure it's the other one that dies."

Jared nodded. "So we kill him. He's a bastard, and Kate," he paused, "— the other Kate — hates him and is being badly used by him. He's dangerous. When he's here, kill him."

Mama Shayga stood up, her back hunched. "It not be dat easy. If he die here in you body, he switch back and you be dead." She pointed a crooked finger at Jared.

Kate threw her arms up, "So we can't do anything! What's the point of all this?"

Kane shook his head. "There isn't much we can do, but maybe we can isolate the occurrences of what is causing the switch and contain J-Rock until the switch back happens. Hopefully, Jared can find a way to make it more difficult for J-Rock back in his own world and it will resolve itself."

"I can't take any more of this at this moment. Kane, please take your friend and leave us alone for a bit." Kate rubbed her forehead and took a deep breath.

Kane nodded, pulled a device from his pocket and reached across the room to hand it to Kate. "If you need me, just press this button and it alerts me you are in trouble."

What am I going to do? she thought, watching as Kane and the old woman left. She turned to look at Jared, who appeared to be in the same state she was.

"I wish I could drink," Kate sighed, and Jared nodded his agreement.

CHAPTER THIRTY-SEVEN

Lessons

I'M GOING TO KILL them, J-Rock thought as he fought the bonds holding him, but then to his relief, they were gone. He flailed his arms in the air and opened his eyes to see Kate hovering over him. J-Rock grabbed her by the throat, threw her to the ground, rolling to press his body to hers, and pinning her to the floor. He felt the pulsing in her neck. It felt good. She tried to scream, but it was no use. Large hands clasped his shoulders. *Mauler? Then that means I'm back*. J-Rock released the grip on his wife's neck and fell back to sit on the floor. Mauler stepped away from him. Kate was gasping for air and holding her neck.

"Kate, I'm sorry. I don't know what's going on. I kind of blanked out." J-Rock rubbed his head, smiling at her as she panted. "But you have to admit you deserved that."

Kate shook her head, her pretty hair falling over her shoulders.

J-Rock got to his feet and paced the room. "Oh, don't give me that shit. I know what you've been plotting. I know all about Detective Kane. So now you're going to tell me what the plan is."

Kate coughed once more and cleared her throat. "I really don't know what you're talking about. I think you're just confused from the seizure you just had."

Stupid bitch, lying again. J-Rock grabbed her hair with both his hands. He imagined her ratting on him to the detective. *She has to be taught not to go against me again.* He yanked her up by her hair. Mauler stepped forward. J-Rock glared back at him.

"Mauler, Kate and I have something to talk about in private." J-Rock nodded to the door.

Mauler hesitated a moment before leaving him and Kate on their own.

J-Rock tightened his grip on Kate's hair and yanked her head back, causing her to yelp.

"Please, honey. Stop. I don't know what you're talking about." Kate reached to stop him from pulling her hair harder, but J-Rock pushed her hand away, pulling with more force.

Watching the tears flow down her pretty face, J-Rock sighed. "Why? I work to give you all of this," he waved his free hand to the room. "Women would die for what you have." He let go of her hair and pushed her to the floor, watching her head hit the tile. She lay still, sobbing, protectively holding her belly. Slowly, he knelt down beside her.

"Kate, I'm not such a bad guy — this is all your fault. I'm doing this for your own good. You don't know how much you hurt me by sneaking around like that." J-Rock reached down and brushed her hair to the side so he could see her cheek. Blood dripped from a gash in her forehead, which he licked. "Poor stupid bitch, but so pretty." He stood back up, still looking down at her. "Do you know what I do with those who rat me out, Kate?" He watched as she shook her head. "They die, and I'm known for my methods — they aren't pleasant. Is that what you want, Kate?"

Kate turned her head up to look at him, "Please. I never said anything. I'm sorry. Please—" J-Rock cut her off by slapping her.

"Shut up! I'm talking. You need discipline, Kate. I didn't ask you to explain yourself. I asked if it was what you wanted. A simple yes or no. What the hell is wrong with you?" J-Rock spat at her. *Women.*

Reaching down, he grabbed her hair once more and pulled. "On your feet."

Kate stood. "Please, the baby. Please don't hurt the baby."

The baby. The baby. All about the baby. Who gives a shit about the baby? It's about respect. No respect for me.

"Kate! Enough! What don't you get? All you care about is that stupid brat growing inside you. You plotted against your own husband, Kate. Me! J-Rock!" he patted his chest to emphasize the matter. "You need a lesson, Kate, and I do this out of love. I'm sure you will come to understand that later." He gripped her hair tighter and led her out to where he stored his favorite golf clubs. Kate tried to squirm away, but J-Rock pushed her to the wall. Her head hit the sheetrock, making a dull thud. She fell back to the floor, grabbing her forehead.

"No, no, no. Please, J-Rock. Our baby," she sobbed.

"Again with the baby." J-Rock pulled out a club and took a deep breath. "Kate, someone has to die here and I love you too much for it to be you. No one goes behind my back."

Kate scrambled to get to her feet, but stumbled. J-Rock grabbed her shoulder, pushed her to her back, and raised the club in the air above his head with the other hand. *It has to be. Someone has to pay. It's probably not even my baby — stupid bitch.* The thought was all he needed to push him further. In one fast swing the club landed with full force in the center of Kate's stomach. Kate shrieked, grasping her belly. She gasped for air and tried to sit up, but J-Rock pushed her down with his foot, raising the club up again. "It's almost over, dear."

He brought the club down again. Kate yelled.

J-Rock smiled down at her. "Maybe this will teach you some respect?"

Yes, this needed to be done. She will learn from this. One more time should do it, he thought as he blocked out the screaming.

Again he hit her with the club, followed by one more for good measure. Throwing the club aside, he reached into his pocket and pulled out his cell phone. He glanced down at his wife, now red and bruised, holding her large belly.

"Kate, I think we need to call a doctor." He walked away and dialed the number for the *family* doctor as he walked to the other room.

Glancing over his shoulder, he watched Kate roll on the floor clutching her belly. The voice of an older man answered his call.

"This is Jim."

"Jim, this is J-Rock. I have a situation that needs your discretion," he paused, "it's my wife."

"I'll be over shortly," the other man replied.

"I think she's miscarried — if she hasn't, she will."

Jim was quiet a moment before responding, "Understood."

J-Rock turned the phone off, walking back to where Kate lay on the floor. She was clutching her belly and gasping for breath in between moans. He shook his head and sighed. "It didn't have to be like this, sweetie."

"Bastard!" Kate spat on his boot. "Our baby!"

"What the hell is it with you? Don't you get it? You went behind my back, you needed this to happen. Maybe now you will finally learn." J-Rock rubbed his temples; he could feel a headache approaching. Too much stress for one day. "Kate, the doctor will be here soon. Please try to keep your moaning and sobbing to a minimum, my head is killing me."

"My poor baby," she gasped as she stared in disbelief at the pool of blood she lay in.

J-Rock rolled his eyes. "Whatever," he muttered as he walked away, making his way to his study, where he settled into his chair. He reached into the desk and withdrew a pair of headphones. *Some music might help — at least it will block out all that damned moaning,* he thought. He started up a playlist of his favorite songs to help him relax; that and a little of his special product, of course.

Chapter Thirty-Eight

Visit

A SHRIEK IN THE still of the night woke Jared from his already fitful sleep. Rubbing his eyes, he cursed himself for staying up so late. The detective and his strange friend, Mama Shayga, had spent the evening discussing what the next options should be for handling the other *him*. They hadn't left until well after midnight. Already spooked by the conversation with Kane and Mama Shayga, the unexpected noise shattered any expectation he had for getting some much-needed sleep.

Listening carefully, no other sounds could be heard besides the occasional rattling of the heater. His heart still pounding from being awoken by the strange noise, he couldn't shake the idea he had actually heard something. Glancing down at Kate, who usually awoke at the slightest noises these days and was still sound asleep, he concluded that it couldn't have been anything — just a dream. *No, I heard it.* Slowly he got out of bed. He was careful not to wake Kate. Glancing down the hall, he saw that baby Lila's door was open. No other sound came from the room. Standing still a moment longer, he tried to remember the details about what it was he had heard. The noise seemed to be an adult woman's voice. Specifically, Kate's voice.

It was so real, he thought. He was about ready to climb back into bed when he heard a creak coming from baby Lila's room. His heart picked up its pace. He tried to swallow his fear.

"I'm being stupid," he muttered, "just the building settling — that's all," he told himself. He crept out of the bedroom to Lila's doorway, peering into the dark room.

The room was completely dark. Jared could make out Lila's crib, empty and waiting for the baby's arrival. Smiling to himself, he started to turn around when he noticed motion from the corner of the room. The rocking chair was moving slightly, as if someone had been sitting in it recently and had just left. *No, it has to be my eyes playing tricks — the darkness maybe. It has to be that — just the dark*, he reassured himself and walked a cautious step at a time into the room. His heart pounded. The chair was moving. *Wind?* he thought as he reached out to stop the chair. A shimmer of light in front of him made him jump back. He squashed a yell by covering his mouth with his hand so not to wake Kate. The light faded. The chair was rocking once more.

"No, no no. That did not just happen!" he told himself under his breath — but it had. The light disappeared completed and Jared shook his head in disbelief. The light returned, this time stronger and brighter. He looked into the light, holding a hand up to shield his eyes. It wasn't lighting up the whole room, but aimed directly at him. Staring into the light was blinding, his eyes having no time to adjust from being in a dark room. What he saw caused him to gasp. Inside the light shimmered. Jared saw the shape of a person — a beautiful woman. It was Kate, and she was holding a baby.

Jared heard a voice in his mind, Kate's voice saying, "Jared, please don't be scared." It reassured him.

Jared stood in place, half wanting to run like hell, but the other half of him — the winning half — wanted to know more of what was going on here, so he stayed.

A baby, unmoving, lay nestled in her arms.

Jared tried to speak, but his voice was still trapped in his throat. The feeling of danger had left, but he couldn't shake the uneasy feeling he was experiencing. *This is Kate, but how?*

"It's me, Kate — J-Rock's Kate," she said, as if reading his thoughts. "J-Rock hurt me and killed my beautiful little baby. I think—" she paused, "I think I'm dying."

The light around Kate began to fade again. She kept talking, but he didn't hear her any longer. It was as though her voice was too great a distance away. Stepping forward, he tried to listen harder, but he couldn't make out any of what she was trying to tell him. Then, as if someone had turned up the volume on a stereo, her voice came back stronger than it had been before it faded.

"The pain, it hurts, it keeps going away and coming back again. I don't think I have much more time here or there," she paused, "but J-Rock needs to be stopped. He will come after you and your family, Jared. You need to kill him."

"How? If I kill him, I might die myself." Jared shook his head. "I don't know what to do."

"Just kill him. Protect your wife and daughter. Find a way and kill him whatever the cost. He's mad, and he won't stop."

"What did he do to you, Kate?" Jared asked and knelt down, peering at the baby, sound asleep in her arms.

"He beat me — I... I can't talk about this, time is short. Mauler has the book and is getting it to Kane. If J-Rock finds out, he'll do anything to get back at you, and that means going after your family."

"Kate, I'm so sorry. I'm sorry I couldn't help you," he said as tears streamed down his cheeks.

"You can still help me. You can help me by killing that bastard and keeping your family safe," she said and began to fade again. This time, instead of fading to darkness, the color around her remained white and then faded to translucent before disappearing all together.

Jared remained still, kneeling near the chair. She was gone.

CHAPTER THIRTY-NINE

The Journal

KANE SAT PATIENTLY IN his car watching people go about their lives in a rush at the Wal-Mart parking lot. It always amazed him how people rushed around to buy the junk they thought they needed. He glanced down at his watch and checked the time. *Late, that can't be good*, he thought and reached down for another chip. Barbecue — the really coated kind that always leaves a bright orange color on anything that comes into contact with them. Kane thought about how his doctor would get at him if he knew about his snack food habit and scowled. *It still beats smoking*. A car pulled into the lot, but it wasn't the Jeep that belonged to Kate. Worry crept into his mind and he unconsciously began munching on more chips until he realized he was at the end of the bag already. A seagull flew overhead, unleashing a runny turd onto his windshield. *Another bad sign*.

Crumpling up the chip bag while sending crumbs across the car seat, Kane let out a sigh of relief to see the Jeep turn into the parking lot and drive to where he was parked. Wiping his hands on his worn jacket, he stepped out of his car and waved to the car. It was the big body guard, Mauler, and not Kate. Mauler looked upset.

The Jeep came to a quick stop in front of Kane's old car. The big man stepped out and glanced at his wristwatch before looking back to where Kane waited. He was rubbing his neck and to Kane's surprise, appeared teary eyed. In the man's hand was a large bound journal spattered with dried blood.

Kane smiled. "Perfect — more evidence," he congratulated himself.

Mauler frowned, "What did you say?"

Kane jumped at the question. "Oh, sorry, I was just muttering. Is that the journal?" he reached his hand out for the book.

Mauler nodded.

Standing awkwardly with his hand outstretched, Kane looked at the bigger man. "May I have it?"

"Kate is in trouble, I don't know if she's OK. I left as soon as J-Rock got home. He started yelling at her the moment he saw her. Kate told me to get this to you, no matter what." Mauler glanced down at the book and then back to Kane. "I did what she asked, but it's not by my choice. I should have stayed with her. Whatever happens to her is on my head."

"You did what you needed to do," Kane said.

"You take this book, and you put him away. If J-Rock finds out Kate and I got this to you, we are as good as dead." Mauler slowly raised the journal to give to Kane.

Kane closed his hand around the journal, but Mauler held tight.

"This better be worth it, Detective."

"Judging by the blood on the front cover and the DNA treasure it holds, I'm sure there is more than enough in here to lock J-Rock away for the rest of time," Kane nodded as he reassured Mauler.

Mauler released his grip on the journal. Kane felt the muscles in his shoulders finally relax. *This is it. Years of investigations and it all comes down to a little journal.* Kane wiped a small tear at the corner of his eye.

It was an odd feeling. A feeling of relief, but also a feeling of sadness that the case he so long wanted to crac, would soon be over. *What's next?* he found himself asking.

Kane walked closer to Mauler, nodding to him. "It's almost over. I'd suggest getting Kate out of the house and disappearing for a few days. I can help with that if you want."

Mauler turned and climbed into his Jeep — the springs creaked at the big man's weight. He looked at Kane, frowning. "Thank you. I'm going back now. If he hurt Kate, I'm not sure he'll be alive for you to arrest any longer." Mauler took a deep breath, "Detective, I have a son. J-Rock has threatened to go after him and J-Rock knows a lot of bad people. He could get it done."

Kane nodded. "I know. I'll make sure your son is protected."

"Thank you, Detective." He didn't wait for the other man's response. He started up the Jeep before driving away, squealing his tires.

Kane watched the Jeep exit the parking lot, and then entered his car. He realized he had barbecue coating on his jacket and shook his head. "Good job," he told himself sarcastically as he opened the journal.

He was right. Inside were the records he needed to put J-Rock away for a very long time. Flipping through the pages, Kane stopped at the last entry in the journal. It followed the last of Slice's entries and was the beginning of J-Rock's writing. J-Rock had jotted down notes about strange occurrences he had experienced frequently. The timing of the occurrences was always around 11:00, both day and night, and he described what appeared to be a different world.

Kane took a deep breath. *Could it be? Could J-Rock really be switching with another person in another world?* He rubbed his chin at the thought, except it wasn't another person; it was J-Rock in another world. Kane laughed. *I really am getting weird in my old age*, he thought and flipped to the next page. It was a drawing of Kate —

except the woman looked slightly different than the Kate that Kane knew. She looked happy. J-Rock had written under the drawing, "I'm coming back, bitch!" in red ink.

Kane closed the journal. If he was right that some mysterious world existed — and he always seemed to be right about weird things — then that would mean that this other woman who looked like the Kate in this world was in danger. J-Rock was more dangerous than he had imagined. Not only was he a threat to Kate and countless others in this realm, he was a threat to innocent people in the *other* realm.

No, it can't be possible. Mama Shayga would have told me if it were. Either I choose to believe it or I don't. He closed his eyes and thought about all the times he had felt as though J-Rock seemed *off* to him. Something else was going on with him than meets the eye. He remembered how often he had felt as though time were different and that the world seemed to be blending with another. Kane never did drugs, so that didn't explain it. He had been told on many occasions that he needed to take medicine for his outlandish thoughts — but he never listened to that advice. *It's the rest of the world that's messed up,* he told himself as he shook off the "I'm crazy" thoughts.

Nodding, he reassured himself of his sanity. "I'm fine. Two worlds do exist — and J-Rock is the link."

He turned the key in the ignition and after a couple tries, the engine came to life. Time to get the backup and take this bastard down — but Kane would have to make sure it was J-Rock, and not the *other* one.

CHAPTER FORTY

Tipping Point

WHAT DID THAT SKANK do with my journal? J-Rock's mind was whirling as he searched his car. It was bad enough that she'd made him her hurt her enough that she'd bled to death in their bed, and now this.

"Damnit! She can rot in hell!" he yelled, slamming the car door. His heart pounded in his chest, thinking about how much damage that journal could do to him if it got in the wrong hands. *She's the only one that could have had any idea where it was,* he thought. He turned and leaned back against the car. The world felt as though it was closing in on him, and it was all Kate's fault. She had found a way to get at him — even after she was dead. His mind drifted to the bittersweet experience of watching her twitch as she passed from life to death — the memory still fresh in his mind.

***

Kate's body had lain still as the old doctor worked — or at least that's what he called himself; J-Rock wasn't sure what he was. All he knew was that he would patch up anyone who had been wounded in some gun fight and would keep his mouth shut about it.

Blood covered the bed. J-Rock had seen many people die from gun wounds or stab wounds, but he had never seen this much blood. Kate would drift in and out of consciousness and would be talking to something or someone no one else saw. Shame for inflicting this upon his wife would creep in as he watched her slowly die at the doctor's hands, but it would quickly be washed away with the anger at her for making him do what he had done to her. The carcass of their lifeless baby boy lay on top of a plastic bag, the placenta still attached. J-Rock thought about how disgusting the thing looked, covered in blood and who knew what else. Kate slipped out one more time as the doctor tried to control the bleeding to no avail.

The old man looked over to J-Rock and shook his head, "I don't think she'll make it. I've done what I can," he said as he reached into the front pocket of his jacket, ignoring the blood smearing across the front as he did so, and pulled a silver flask. He removed the cap and took a good sip before handing the flask to J-Rock.

J-Rock took a swig. Burning its way down his throat, the alcohol felt good. He needed something to calm down his nerves. J-Rock nodded to the old man. "You did what you could. She was becoming too much of a pain anyway. I can get better than her now." He handed the flask back and the 'doctor' took another swig.

The old man waved his arm, sweeping it across the room. "This is going to take some time to clean. I can get a crew in here to take care of the body," he paused and then glanced down at the little figure on the floor, "bodies."

J-Rock smiled and stepped forward to pat the old doctor on the back. "You do good work."

As he turned to leave, a gasp erupted from Kate's lips. J-Rock turned to face her. Her eyes were shut, but she was saying something very quietly, with whatever strength or life she had left. J-Rock cautiously stepped forward and leaned to her mouth to listen.

"Kill the bastard. Whatever it takes. Kill him..." her breathy voice faded and she was gone.

J-Rock stepped back and looked over at the doctor, who was as surprised as he was that she'd still had some life left. "Shit. Just finish her off, would you?" J-Rock felt his hands starting to fidget. Slamming the door shut, he left the room on his way to search for his journal.

***

J-Rock sat and stared at the ceiling of the garage. *Whatever it takes. Kill him. What did she mean by that? Who was she talking to? Could she be talking to someone in the other world?* J-Rock laughed to himself. The idea was crazy. Crazy, but he had switched to the other world frequently — and he knew it was real. Sure, psychiatrists would have a fun time listening to his story and he might get some good drugs out of it, legally!

It would be just like her to do that to me. The light above flickered and he heard rummaging from inside the house. Deep voices expressed their disgust at the sight. The cleaners had arrived, which was all well and good. The sooner Kate's body was out of the house the better. Maybe then he'd stop with these stupid thoughts. As hard as he tried, the thought that Kate had been speaking to someone in another space kept nagging at him. *Maybe she was talking to the other Kate. Or maybe the other him! How can I kill me, though? I never see myself. He switches with me.*

"I am losing it," he thought out loud, listening to his own voice echo in the garage as he sat next to his car. "I'll just kill the *other* Kate. Then maybe the *other* me will kill himself with grief." He snickered.

I'll just chip away at him every time I switch. I can't be tried for murder in a world that I hardly exist in — I can make it look like it was him and he'll end up in prison. He smiled at how much fun he could have.

Feeling relieved that he had developed a plan of action, he took a deep breath and stood. Lights were visible through the window in the garage door. It was Kate's Jeep. He watched Mauler step out and rush to the entrance. *Oh, good. Kate's lover is back,* he thought as he reached into the car, pulling out his revolver. He checked to make sure it was loaded. Of course it was. Smiling at how efficient he was, he put the gun in his sport coat pocket and walked back to the living room to meet Mauler, who was questioning the cleaners as they worked on the stain in the carpet. When he saw J-Rock enter, he gave him a look seething with anger. It was a look J-Rock loved to see right before he killed someone. *Good. Go to hell with that hate,* he thought as Mauler asked him in his deep voice, "Where's Kate?"

J-Rock casually walked forward, but stopped just far enough away that Mauler wouldn't be able to attack him and cause any bodily damage. The two men cleaning the carpet in the middle of the room glanced up at J-Rock and he nodded at them to leave. They gathered up their equipment, leaving in a matter of seconds. *I'll have to thank the Doc for such a good cleaning team.*

"Why so much concern for Kate? I thought you worked for me," J-Rock asked.

"What did you do to her? Is she OK?" Mauler stepped forward slowly.

"Oh, no worries. You can see her in a minute." He smiled back.

"I'm not doing this anymore. I'm getting out and I'm taking Kate with me. You won't hurt her anymore — I won't let you."

J-Rock laughed. "Oh, you can take Kate with you. I don't care." He withdrew the gun from his pocket and held it to his side. "You and Kate can have all the fun in the world together. First, you need to tell me where my journal is."

Motion to the right caught both men by surprise as a couple of men hauled something heavy and wrapped in a black bag out of the bedroom. A third man held a smaller bag. Not knowing what had been taking place in the living room, the movers looked as surprised as J-Rock and Mauler were. Mauler ran to them and ripped the larger bag open. He held his head in his hands a moment, gasping. He ripped the bag free of the men's grips and the it fell to the floor.

"Kate! No! Kate!" he sobbed and looked up at J-Rock. "You will pay for this. How could you do this?" Tears dripped down his face as he ripped free the bag wrapped around Kate's head, cradling her head in his arms, brushing away the strands of hair on her face. He looked back to J-Rock and shook his head. "You are pure evil. Why? Why would you do this? She was pregnant, with your—" he paused and looked at the other man holding the smaller bag, about the size of a small dog. "Is that...?" he couldn't get the rest of his question out.

J-Rock laughed at the man, crying like a baby on the floor. "Yes, it's Kate and her whelp." He waved the gun around as he spoke. "To be honest, I don't even know if it was my baby she had. I wouldn't be surprised if she was selling herself on the street." He paused and stepped another step closer. "Now tell me where that journal is!"

Mauler gently set Kate's head down on the floor, then stood up, wiping his tears away. "I've seen a lot of death, but what you did here," he motioned to the body on the floor and the small bag, still held by one of the cleaners, "this is too much."

J-Rock shook his head, "I don't care what you think, Mauler. Tell me where that journal is or you are as dead as your son will be."

Mauler's face reddened and he charged. Quicker than J-Rock ever imagined the big man could be, he almost made it close enough to hit him. J-Rock casually took a step back, firing a shot into the man's leg. Mauler stumbled to the floor. J-Rock kicked him in the stomach and Mauler rolled onto his back, gasping for air.

"Tell me where that journal is and this will be over. You can be with my whore, Kate, just like you wanted." J-Rock walked over to tell the movers to leave and come back later with another bag and more cleaning supplies. They nodded and hurried out. Mauler and J-Rock were alone in the room.

Mauler was able to lift himself to a crouch. *It's going to be hard finding a replacement for him,* J-Rock thought, jumping back as Mauler lunged forward once again. J-Rock hit him in the side of his head with the butt of the pistol. The sound of metal against the man's head made for a satisfying cracking sound. Mauler stumbled forward, but he kept his balance. Blood drenched the jeans around his large leg where he had been shot. He turned to face J-Rock, his face still flushed. J-Rock watched as the man wavered, but still held his balance. Blood dripped down the side of Mauler's face where a gash had opened up from the hit he had taken.

"You just don't get it, do you? I thought you were a smart guy," J-Rock said and fired a shot in the other leg.

Mauler fell to the floor once more, but he wasn't giving up yet.

J-Rock walked closer to kick him again. Mauler lunged at him again. *This guy is a juggernaut,* he thought, as Mauler wrapped his arms around him and brought him crashing to the ground on his back. Half dazed, J-Rock fired a shot randomly. It missed Mauler's head by a few inches. Mauler gripped J-Rock's neck and squeezed. Blood from the giant man's open wound dripped down into his face. *Shit, he's going to kill me,* he thought as he struggled for breath.

Mauler smiled at him. "This is what I do, J-Rock. This is my job. Except this time, I get to kill who I want to kill."

His vision fading, J-Rock struggled, but Mauler's weight was too much for him to get any leverage. *No, I can't die like this. Not from this meathead.*

Gasping with no relief, J-Rock felt his vision fading one last time, when another shot was fired. *Was that me?* The sound was very faint, or at least that's how it sounded to him as he struggled for air. A surge of breath broke past the blockage he had been fighting. The air was cool. He gasped and rolled to his side. A shiny pair of shoes stood in front of him. Straining to look up, he saw it was the old 'doctor'. He glanced down at where J-Rock lay at his feet and reached down to help him stand. Mauler was next to him, bleeding from his shoulder, and trying to stand. The doctor hit the bigger man in the head with the butt of his handgun. Mauler fell to the floor, unconscious.

"I'm more than a doctor, you know" he said, matter-of-factly.

J-Rock panted for air and rubbed his neck. "No, I didn't know that."

The doctor helped steady him. "I used to be like him," he pointed to where Mauler lay on the floor, finally passed out. "Well, not as big as him. Years in the military as a field doctor, I learned a lot about killing. Except, I'm not as good a shot as I used to be."

J-Rock shook his head, "Well, I'm glad you didn't decide to turn on your boss too."

Jumping at the noise from tires grinding to a stop and blue lights shining into the room, J-Rock was spurred into action.

"That's where my journal went, I guess. Better get a move on, Doc, I think I need to get out of the country."

The doctor, nodding, slowly walked to the rear of the house where the back door was. J-Rock, limping to the intercom on the wall next to the door, issued commands to his guards, "Take them out."

Machine gun fire echoed through the air as the guards posted on the roof of the house began firing at the police. *This is it, the big one*, J-Rock thought, entering his armory closet. Dressing himself in a protective vest, he glanced down at his watch. *Perfect, just a little longer*, he thought and smiled. He withdrew a machine gun, strapping it around him, and then pulled out a shotgun. He loaded the shotgun and pumped it. Grabbing a gas mask, he closed the closet and turned to face the invasion. "Let's get this over with!"

Chapter Forty-One

Sacrifice

KANE WATCHED AS THE police descended upon the mansion. He was at a safe distance to observe the situation unfold. As expected, gunfire erupted, forcing the police back into a defensive position. The way this was headed, they'd be pinned, allowing J-Rock to slip away under the cover of chaos. A media helicopter circled in the sky. Kane glanced down at his watch, noting the time. If J-Rock played his cards right, he'd make the switch and the wrong person would get caught — or worse, killed. *I need to get to him before it's too late.*

Kane sighed and got out of his car, slipping on a protective vest. Staying low, he ran to the armored tactical van where the captain in charge of the raid was giving orders.

"Detective, get back and let my guys take care of this," the captain shouted at him.

Kane shook his head. He never had liked dealing with the regular police force. He knew the captain thought he was loony. The only reason the Captain kept him around was because he felt bad for him since his loss years ago — well, that and his weird way of solving cases that no one else could solve.

"Captain, I need to get in there as soon as possible," he shouted over the nearby gun fire. "If I don't get in there, I'm afraid the situation could get really bad."

The captain scowled and spat on the ground. "Worse? How can it get worse? We're taking a lot of gunfire from — I don't know how many bad guys — and you're telling me it could get worse?" He took a deep breath. "Kane, go home. You did good. You got what we needed, now let us do our job and finish what you started for us."

"Look, the guy we're after is going to get out. The longer we sit here, the longer he has to find a way out. He's a smart guy; don't give him the chance," Kane told the captain, exasperation in his voice.

"What's the plan, Detective? How do you expect to get past all of this?" He asked.

"I just need a little cover. Shoot some gas into the room with some smoke. I'll sneak around the side and search for him," Kane pleaded.

"Detective, I like you — even with your eccentricities, but you aren't Rambo. You're not even Elmer Fudd. More like Mr. Magoo, except you see slightly better." The captain turned away and started issuing orders for the sharpshooters.

Kane reached out, pulling him back one last time. "Please, Captain. Give me this. J-Rock needs to be brought down and it needs to happen now! Just give me a little smoke and some cover."

The captain rolled his eyes and began to protest, but Kane cut him off. "I promise, do this for me, and I'll retire after. You won't have to put up with me anymore. Please. I have nothing and I need to bring this gang down — for my family."

"All right, Kane. We'll get you some cover. But you're taking this on yourself. If you get killed, it's your own damned fault." The captain radioed the order to fire off some smoke and gas around the premises and into the windows.

"Thank you, Captain!"

Before Kane could run, the captain patted his shoulder. "Be careful, Kane."

Kane nodded, keeping low as he ran closer to the house, staying crouched, running from car to car. A shot bounced off the back of a vehicle just as he crouched down behind it. *I'm as loony as people think I am*, he thought, as smoke cans began covering the area with a dark fog. Windows crashed as cans of gas were shot into the building. *Now!* Kane kept low and ran to the side of the mansion, climbing in through a broken window. He felt his pants rip slightly in the crotch. *Brilliant!* He slipped down to the floor, crouching low, looking around the room and letting his eyes adjust. He was in the garage. A sleek red Ferrari and an armored Hummer sat parked in the bay.

Carefully, he moved around the car, and then entered the room connected to the garage. Heart pounding, Kane moved from wall to wall. The entryway led to a spacious family room. A large black bag lay in the center of the room, near which Kane saw a slumped body. It was Mauler. Glancing around the room to make sure no one else was around, he ran closer to where Mauler lay sprawled on the floor and checked his pulse. It was faint, but he was alive. Kane looked over to see Kate's face protruding from the black bag. *Too late*, he thought and moved on. *This is my only chance to get J-Rock.*

As Kane was about to rise, he turned to see the man he was after on the other side of the room, wearing a mask and pointing a shotgun at him. Not hesitating a moment, Kane ducked behind an overturned couch just as J-Rock fired off a shot. The sound was loud. Stuffing from the couch flew into the air. Kane drew his pistol as he kept behind the couch and fired two shots, sending J-Rock into cover.

"I hope you saw what you made me do to your informers. Now you can join them," J-Rock shouted out and fired another shot, sending more stuffing into the air.

"There is nowhere to go. It's over. Give up and you can live through this, son," Kane shouted back and glanced again at his watch. Time was running out. What he'd just told J-Rock was a lie. Kane would kill him. It was the only way that others could be safe.

J-Rock fired another shot. Kane peeked over the couch to see him bolting for the door across the room, leading to the garage. Kane stood up, firing a shot that nicked J-Rock in the shoulder. Grabbing his shoulder, J-Rock turned to fire a return from the shotgun. The shot hit the top of the couch, sending fragments back at Kane.

Stumbling back, Kane fell to the floor, shielding his eyes. J-Rock laughed and threw down the shotgun. He withdrew the machine gun strapped over his shoulder and aimed at Kane, firing a round. It was a wild shot. Kane could tell he was having a hard time holding the gun. J-Rock's wound was slowing him down. Kane crawled for cover. He lost his grip on his gun and it slid across the floor. *Shit, it's over now,* he thought as he sat in the open, nothing nearby to provide adequate cover. J-Rock walked closer, a smile on his face.

"Looks like you lose, Detective. I've wanted to do this for a long time." J-Rock raised the gun to take aim. Kane stared at him, hatred burning inside of him.

POP! POP!

Kane flinched.

Expecting pain or blackness, Kane jumped to hear a shriek of agony that was not his own. It was coming from where J-Rock stood. J-Rock fell back, the gun dropping to the ground, his hand covered in blood. *Where did that shot come from?* Kane turned to see Mauler, wounded by a wild shot from J-Rock, who had been aiming for Kane. The large man lay bleeding from his neck and quivering. Kane's revolver rested in his hand.

J-Rock stumbled through the open door to the garage. Kane heard him starting up his car. Kane grabbed his revolver from the big man's bloodied hand. "Thank you, Mauler. I'll make sure your son is all right". Mauler gasped for one more breath before lying still. Kane followed where J-Rock had exited.

Gun shots from the battle outside raged on, but it sounded as though more shots were being fired from the ground up, which meant the police were getting closer. Heart pounding, Kane reached the garage. J-Rock was in the SUV. Kane fired a shot at the driver's window, but it ricocheted. *Armored. Damnit!* Kane spat. It didn't matter, J-Rock couldn't back out of the garage anyway. The police had blocked the area off.

What Kane saw next, he would not have believed possible. J-Rock drove the SUV through the front of the garage. At first, it did not make it all the way through, but refusing to be captured, J-Rock backed the car and rammed the wall again. Sheetrock and splinters crashed on the hood. Once more, he backed the car and then drove through the opening. Debris that had fallen on the hood showered the garage. Kane ran after, firing shots at the car, knowing it was a fruitless attempt, but more so did it out of frustration. Shouting after him, Kane wiped away sweat on his forehead.

"Dammit! I failed!" he shouted and fell to the ground as he gasped for breath.

No, you haven't failed. But this time, it wasn't his voice. It was a woman's voice. *Get your ass up and go get him,* the voice nagged him. It was a voice he hadn't heard for a long time — his wife's voice. *Make that son of a bitch pay!* she yelled. Kane stood up, shaking off the dirt from his backside. The tear in his pants was quite large now.

"All right. I'm not done yet," he said to the cool air, turning to get back to his car. He found a white towel in the garage to wave at the police, who were firing at anything that was currently moving. Taking a deep breath, he stepped out of the garage. He tried not to mess himself.

Chapter Forty-Two

Running Man

Laughing as the SUV crashed through the fence at the edge of the property, J-Rock felt the blood-coated steering wheel slip in his grip. Blood was dripping from the wound in his hand. A few policemen jumped back as the fence shattered and sent shards of splinters into the air. A lucky shot bounced off the bulletproof glass in front of J-Rock's eyes and he jumped back. He laughed again. The exhilaration of the day was overwhelming. Who knew this could be so much fun?

J-Rock swerved the car around the parked police vehicles. He glanced in his rearview mirror to see confused policemen watch the SUV maneuver the obstacles and make its escape.

Shoulder burning and throbbing, J-Rock pushed the pain aside, focusing on picking up speed. The engine whirred and the road was clear. *So easy!* he thought and glanced at his watch. *Not much longer now.* The police had yet to catch up to him as they ran for their cars. J-Rock looked down at his pants covered in blood from where his hand rested on his leg. Raising a bloody finger, he leaned forward to write a message on the window with his own blood.

Between his writing and driving, J-Rock saw an old rusty car in his mirror. It was picking up speed, getting closer, shimmying, and barely able to keep from falling apart. *Kane!* he thought. He was the only one stupid enough to be driving at such speed with a crap car like that. J-Rock slammed the brakes, hoping the other car would swerve off the road or crash into the back of his SUV. Kane swerved around easily, slowing down to match the SUV's speed. J-Rock turned to see Kane pointing his revolver at him and firing. Like the other shot, this one bounced harmlessly off the glass, leaving only a small chip. J-Rock smiled back, swinging the steering wheel to the left to hit his pursuer's car.

Kane's car swerved. Kane nearly drove into the ditch on the other side of the road. To J-Rock's dismay, the old man kept it on the road, veering back into the right lane behind him. *Just give it up, old man!* he thought. J-Rock saw a parade of blue flashing lights not far behind Kane. He looked at his watch once more. This was his only chance. He had never commanded a switch before. A roadblock had been set up ahead. J-Rock swerved the car onto a side road. *They are routing me into a trap*, he thought and searched for an alternate route. The highway was not far from him, but the roadblock was preventing him from getting to the entrance. "I'll just have to make my own," he said to himself.

He was on a small side road. An old path for ATVs was approaching on his right. Kane still lagged behind, avoiding potholes as best he could. His car wouldn't be able to keep pace much longer. J-Rock turned onto the old path, his SUV barely fitting between the trees and brush. The SUV bounced as he ran over the branches and roots covering the path. *Either this will lead me to another road, or it will be my end.* He still needed to hold out a little while longer.

The path grew narrower, with branches scraping the side of the SUV. His hand pulsing, J-Rock was beginning to feel a little light-headed. It was surprising how much blood loss a small bullet wound could cause. A helicopter flew overhead. J-Rock peered at the sky to see if it was the police or media, but he couldn't see through the thick trees overhead. Kane had either decided not to follow on the trail or his car was stuck. The trail ahead was covered in mud. J-Rock had nowhere else to go but forward.

Just need a little more time. He savored the thought of making his double pay dearly for the trouble he had caused. Switching to four-wheel drive, J-Rock plowed the SUV through the mud with no problem.

The helicopter still hovered overhead, but he doubted it could see him under all the tree cover. Pushing forward, he could see the trail opening up to another side road.

"HA!" he yelled as he approached the end of the trail.

With no cops in sight, he pulled onto the road and headed in the direction of the highway, which he could now see clearly. A small gully blocked the road from the highway. He stopped short of the gully and looked around to make sure no police were nearby yet. There were none. Reaching into the glove compartment, he withdrew a bag of cocaine. As he inhaled the powder, he thought, *Might as well enjoy what's left.* The rush hit him in a giant wave. He floored the gas pedal, pushing the SUV into and over the gully.

The turnpike was practically empty. The helicopter easily tracked him now. He rolled down the window, flipping the eye in the sky as he got on the turnpike. Nothing could stop him. His heart racing as he passed other cars, he felt invincible. Glancing down at his watch, he saw he had only had another few minutes. Sirens wailed in the background and the wind from the open window blew through his hair. He closed his eyes. It was amazing. He took his hands off the wheel. *Now or never. Come to my world.* He smiled, picturing the little kitchen belonging to his other self. He pictured Kate, alive and well, arms around her pregnant belly. Then, the pull. It was working. He focused harder. The chaotic world he knew vanished and he found himself lying on the floor of a living room. He opened his eyes and saw Kate. She had a gun. It was pointed at him.

CHAPTER FORTY-THREE

The Final Switch

"OH MY GOD!" JARED shouted when he saw the tail end of a car fly to his right after hitting it with the SUV that he was driving. Grabbing the steering wheel, he fought to keep control of the speeding vehicle. Swerving right and left, he brought the car back under control and slowed down. Sirens rang from behind him. A helicopter thundered above. Slowly he pulled into the breakdown lane. His head was flying and his heart pounded, but he felt *good*. Glancing down at the passenger seat, he could see white powder and an empty sandwich bag. *Coke?* He glanced back at the windshield, where J-Rock had written a message in what appeared to be blood.

Kate, mine!

Jared panicked. Turning, he saw a sea of blue lights approaching, fast. His coat pocket vibrated. He reached into his pocket to find a cell phone. Jared fumbled with the phone to answer the call.

"This is Kane!" He sounded winded. Sirens screamed in the background.

"Kane? What the hell is happening?"

"Look, I know what your situation is. No time, but you need to drive."

"Where? Why are the police after me?"

A voice on a loudspeaker from the helicopter instructed him to get out of the car with his hands behind his head.

"No time. Just drive. If you get caught, I can't guarantee you'll be safe," Kane said.

Jared frantically turned to see that the police were almost upon him.

"Shit!" He floored the gas pedal and the SUV picked up speed.

"Kane, you still there?"

"I'm here, but I have to go. Just keep driving and keep your phone handy," he paused a moment. "I'll call when I can," Kane said and then disconnected.

Jared yelled in frustration. His heart still pounded and everything around him seemed so slow. "Stupid car! Can't this thing go any faster?" He pressed the gas pedal harder. The speedometer needle was fixed at 100. The SUV shimmied. Thankfully, the road was empty.

Kate. I have to get back to Kate, he thought and kept driving. He didn't know where he'd go or what to do. A tear dripped down his cheek. *If he hurts her — SHUT UP! Get back to her. I need to focus! But if he hurts her — I SAID, SHUT UP!* He hit his head with his hand.

At that moment, he realized it was the source of all the blood on the window. Jared glanced at his hand; a chunk on the side near his pinky had a gaping wound. *Huh?* he thought and focused his attention back to the road. His shoulder pulsed. He had no time to examine his body any further. His mind raced. *Coke.*

The sirens appeared to be farther behind now and the helicopter fell back slightly. Jared frowned. *Why would they be backing off?* The phone buzzing cut his thoughts off.

He picked it up and answered, "Yes?"

"Jared, it's Kane."

"Tell me what the hell to do! I'm freaking out!" Jared yelled.

"Calm down. Just slow down and pull to the side."

"No way. They'll kill me. I'm pumped up with coke! Shit! I'm on coke!"

"It's OK. Just pull over. I bought us some time — I said I needed some time with you and I could get you to stop."

"I don't do drugs. I've never done drugs. The cops — they'll kill me, won't they?"

"No one is going to kill you, just pull over."

Jared hadn't realized that he was slowing down already. He pulled the car to the side and slowed to a stop. "OK, I pulled over."

"I'm on my way. Hang tight," Kane said.

Turning to see an older car driving towards him, he asked. "Is that you? In the old car?"

"Yes, that's me."

The car approached and came to a stop behind him. Kane got out of his car, his hands in the air to show he didn't have a gun. Jared, sighing slowly, opened the door. Standing, his head felt heavy and he thought he might faint.

Kane, stopping short of Jared, motioned for him to stay still. Kane nodded toward the helicopter. "They have a gun targeting you right now. It's best if we have some distance between us so we don't lead them to think I'm in danger."

Jared could feel his blood pressure rising. *This is it. I'm going to die here,* he thought and tried to focus instead on living. "I need to get back to Kate."

"I know. You must focus on getting back, Jared," he said.

"I can't do that. I have to wait until it brings me back."

Kane shook his head. "No, it needs to be now. I know it sounds crazy, but I'm feeling a strong imbalance this hour of the day lately. J-Rock caused the switch. You should be able to do the same."

"How? I don't know how to do it."

"Focus, Jared. Focus on your life back home." Kane turned to look back at the empty highway and then to the helicopter above. "You need to do it, Jared. You need to do it now."

Jared closed his eyes, visualizing his apartment. He visualized Kate. The pulling sensation began, ever so slightly, but it felt as though he was being fought. *J-Rock,* he thought. He tried again. The thundering of the helicopter faded to a slight hum. Faintly, he could see Kate holding a gun pointed at him, and then the drum of the helicopter became stronger again. He focused harder.

He was back at his apartment, but for only a moment. Then he was back standing in front of Kane, but now his hand was in his jacket pocket and resting on something cold. A gun! Kane had his gun drawn. Beads of sweat dotted Kane's forehead. He kept glancing up at the helicopter. Then the detective was running forward, leaping towards him. A loud crack sounded from the sky above. Jared felt the weight of Kane's body plow into him. Kane gasped as they both fell to the ground. Kane rolled to his side. Blood covered his right shoulder. Jared scrambled to rest his back against the tire of the SUV. *Shit. They are going to kill me, here in this world,* he thought as he glanced back to Kane. Kane's hand still rested on the gun. Kane looked back at him.

"Last time, Jared. It's now or never"

Jared nodded, closing his eyes and focusing as hard as he could. The scene began to fade. He was transferring again. As J-Rock's world faded, he thought he heard a gunshot.

CHAPTER FORTY-FOUR

Peace

KANE WATCHED CAREFULLY AS Jared closed his eyes and tried to switch again. J-Rock was not going down without a fight — which he expected would be the case. He glanced at the helicopter as it turned around to get a better angle for a shot. *Come on Jared, focus. Time is slipping,* he thought as he exhaled. The wound in his shoulder was sending waves of pain through his side. He desperately fought passing out. Kane could see a white cloud slowly leaving Jared's body and then slipping back. Again, it slowly began to rise. Slightly above, he could see a darker apparition getting pulled towards the body. A dark and twisted voice entered Kane's thoughts: *Detective, what are you doing? I will kill you. Slice took out your family, now I'll finish the job and take you out as well.* Kane pushed away the voice and waited.

The helicopter had made a full circle and was getting closer, lining up for a good shot, free of obstructions. The white apparition finally drifted free of the body, fading out of view as the dark cloud descended into J-Rock's body. Kane pulled the trigger. The bullet entered J-Rock's forehead and banged against the side of the SUV. A stream of blood dripped down from where the bullet made its hole. A shriek echoed in Kane's mind: *NO! You can't have. This can't happen!*

The black mist vanished, leaving no trace of its existence. Kane let his head fall as he slipped out of consciousness. He had done what he could do. The rest was up to Jared.

CHAPTER FORTY-FIVE

Life Continues

JARED'S VISION RETURNED. HE was back at the apartment where Kate stood over him, ready to kill him, if need be. It was the agreement they had made. Kane stood next to her.

"It's him again," Kane told her, pushing her arm down to point the gun at the floor.

This time there was no pull back. He was home. Jared smiled at Kate. "It's me, Kate. I'm home." He glanced at Kane. "You saved us, Kane. In the other world, you helped me."

Kane frowned. "Well, I'm glad I could help — again."

Jared rolled over and Kate undid the bonds holding his hands together. They hadn't wanted to leave anything to chance. Hands free, Jared stood, embracing Kate, squeezing her tight. "We're safe now."

He didn't notice the dark shadow staring back into the room from the mirror. A dark shadow wanting nothing but revenge, forced to wander between two worlds, having a home in neither.

Chapter Forty-Six

Mama's Revenge

Mama Shayga watched as Kane set down the grocery bag. She smiled at him. *Such a good man. He's taken care of me all these years.*

"I brought you some goodies, Mama." Kane smiled back. "The young man testified today. Slice is behind bars.""

"Sit Shuga, sit. Have some din wid me." Mama motioned to the pile of cushions set up as makeshift chair.

I have other things to do right now, Kane, she thought. *I'll have to play the 'crazy' card again.*

Kane's face twisted slightly. She could tell he was thinking of some way to slip out before she passed on some rotten food for him to eat.

"No thank you, Mama. The family is waiting for me at home. I wanted to thank you for your help," he smiled and started to make for his exit.

"Shuga! Plenty of leftovers!"

Kane backed further and waved. "Take care, Mama."

Mama watched him leave the alley before turning to the operation she had set up behind the tent. A small fire was burning brightly. Stones had been circled neatly around the fire. She sat down cross-legged and waited. It wouldn't be much longer now.

The air began to feel heavier and dense with water. A thunderstorm was brewing — a storm similar to the one when Jared was a young man.

Rain began pelting the ground, but it did not affect the fire. The fire began to burn blue. Mama began chanting. It was a chant passed on to her by her mother. It had probably been passed on to her by *her* mother. It was likely passed on by a poor woman before being sentenced to death by the flames.

Thunder crashed in the distance.

Mama's eyes remained closed, even when the shape appeared beside her.

"You? I'll kill you!" the dark form whispered.

Mama continued her chant.

The shape wrapped its dark hands around her neck. Mama strained, but she continued.

Lighting lit the sky and the flames of blue burned brighter. Mama gasped for air, but none would come. The dark form of J-Rock laughed as he felt Mama's strength fading. She continued, straining for every word that escaped her mouth.

"What are you doing, crazy lady?" J-Rock asked.

Mama opened her eyes. They burned red. She grabbed the apparition's hands. J-Rock fell back, screaming.

"You burned me? How? What are you?" he shrieked.

Mama felt strong. The storm channeled into her. Debris from the alley swirled around her. "You killed me in your world. You have no place any longer." She stood tall.

J-Rock slipped back. "You will not kill me!"

He lunged for Mama as she raised her hands into the air. Before he could get to her, Mama swung them down. A bolt of lightning struck the blue flames, sending bits of flame outward. J-Rock wrapped his wraithlike arms around the old woman, but his arms burned from her touch and disappeared into nothingness. He howled in pain. With the palm of her hand, Mama pushed J-Rock back into the blue flames. Horrible, guttural sounds erupted from the fire.

Mama waved her arms over the fire, and the blue flames disappeared, leaving a pile of black tar like goo. She reached into her robes and withdrew a glass flask. Kneeling down, she scooped the goo into the jar. She ignored the rain pelting down on her. She tightened the cap and walked to her tent.

Inside, she pushed away a heap of fabric to uncover an ancient chest — the only possession of hers that she cared about. The hinges creaked as she opened it. Inside were hundreds of jars, all filled with black goo. She smiled as she added the new jar to the collection.

As she closed the lid of the chest, J-Rock's faint scream could be heard.

"Shhh...There, there." She patted the top of the chest. "When I'm tired, I'll add you to some coffee. We'll be friends for a long time. No one hurts Mama."

Now, what goodies did my sweet Kane bring me?

Conduit: The Beginning Sample

Begin your next journey into the unknown with a sample from Conduit: The Beginning.

JACK SQUEEZED ADRIANNA'S HAND and smiled as she smiled back at him. It always amazed him how he managed to get such a beautiful family. Adrianna's blond hair hung down over her shoulders. It had been a long time that the two of them had gotten to get out of the house since the birth of their newborn daughter, Ashley. A car moved in front of him and directed his attention back to driving. The exit for his job was approaching, and he realized he had his blinker on and he was already in the lane to leave the highway.

"Jack, where are you going?" Adrianna asked with a smile.

"I know, I went on autopilot." Jack switched the blinker on to get in the right lane and veered back on to the highway. A horn sounded behind him and he muttered under his breath.

"Seriously, can't anyone have any patience?" Adrianna turned and flipped the bird to the upset motorist behind them. The car behind honked in return. She turned to sit back in her seat and adjusted her belt. "People!"

Jack laughed. "It was my fault. I did cut him off."

"I know, but it's not like he's any later. He could have just let you back in without having a hissy fit."

The man passed by and returned the hand gesture. Jack smiled back and the car sped off.

Jack took a deep breath and rubbed his eyes. *These late hours at my stupid job are killing me.*

Adrianna glanced at him, her face creased with worry. "You can't keep working so hard. It's catching up with you. Maybe it's time to find something else?"

"Like what? No one is hiring right now. I could wind up with something worse."

"Worse than working seventy hours a week? Or driving every day to a job you despise?"

"There aren't many jobs I wouldn't despise."

Adrianna nodded, "True."

The sign for the mall exit approached. Traffic was surprisingly busy for the weekend. The news began to play on the radio, and Jack turned the volume up to catch the weather. The newscaster was stuck on a segment of the latest hot news about a grisly murder in another state. It had caught the country in shock at how a thirteen-year-old boy could murder his father.

"What the hell is wrong with the world?" Jack shook his head.

"Well, I understand the boy was being abused badly. I suppose he snapped." Adrianna replied over the noise of the radio and the fan.

The reporter began to dig into the details of the murder and Jack switched the station, shaking his head.

More news was playing. It seemed finding any music was a fruitless endeavor.

"There are some out there who really believe aliens have visited Earth many times," the radio disk jockey proceeded to mock the latest news referring to crop circles and alien sightings.

One thing is for sure, there is no shortage of nutjobs out there. He snickered to himself. *At least this is a break from murder and politics.*

The jockey continued, "So, what I want to know is, how many of you listeners have been abducted — perhaps probed and prodded. I mean, are you people for real?"

Well, better than kids murdering their parents.

"Caller, you're on the air."

"Good afternoon. What makes you think people who believe in alien visitations are any less sane than you?" the man's voice was gruff.

"Well, how about the stupid stories of abductions, crop circles, etc. Why the hell would aliens bother with that bogus stuff? I mean, c'mon! Wouldn't you just invade and make yourself emperor, and have a bunch of slave girls at your feet, rather than mess around carving circles in the fields?" the disk jockey responded.

"Consider this: Would you invade a country without first researching it to determine the likelihood of success, the costs, and the benefits? It seems to me any species intelligent enough to arrive here would invest time in various forms of research before taking a risk that would jeopardize the success of the operation."

HONK!

Jack changed lanes to avoid colliding with the woman weaving in and out of traffic as she talked on her cell and drank whatever iced coffee concoction she held in her hand. *Shit! Stupid drivers!*

Ashley stirred from her sleep in the back seat and Adrianna reached back to reassure the baby that all was fine.

"I would have hoped you would have been more open-minded," the caller responded. "Obviously you spend too much time talking and not enough thinking. How would you explain the unexplainable? How would you explain the pyramids, Stonehenge, the Mayan calendar? All things way beyond the technology of the times. Where is your curiosity?"

Good point, I guess. Still a wack job though. Jack found a parking spot at the mall parking lot.

Adrianna opened the door and glanced at the ground. "You parked a little crooked."

Jack gritted his teeth. "It's fine. I'm in the lines."

"OK, don't complain when the guy next to you hits our car with his door."

"Go ahead in, I'll straighten the car out and meet you."

"OK, I'll be in the food court. I'm starving." He watched her head towards the mall entrance with Ashley in her carriage and began to straighten the car.

A man walked in front of him as he moved the car forward slightly and he slammed on the brakes. Jack threw his hands in the air and the man flipped him off. He looked disheveled and wore a long green trench coat. It was torn in several places. He continued walking in the same direction Adrianna and Ashley had gone. The back of the man's coat had a strange emblem Jack had never seen before. There was some text under it, but it was in a language he could not recognize. The man limped and was muttering to himself. *Fucking wacko.* Jack finished parking the car and stepped out. The air was hot and sticky. Much too hot for the outfit the crazy man was wearing.

Just walking to the entrance of the mall was draining. The heat and humidity sapped all motivation for doing anything. Jack just wanted to be in air conditioning, out of the relentless heat. As he opened the door, the cool air rushed out to greet him, promising relief from the summer air. Jack spotted Adrianna moving the baby carriage forward and back as she scanned a menu on a board and walked to meet up with them.

"What are you going to get?" Jack asked, glancing at the menu.

"I was thinking about a salad. You?"

"Probably a bacon burger."

Adriana glared at him. He could feel her gaze burning him.

"What?"

"Seriously?" She patted his gut. "A bacon burger."

"I need the sustenance."

"Didn't you just say you were going to start dieting again?"

"I didn't say when. I just said I would start soon...I'm hungry."

"You need to think about your health. But do whatever you want!" Adrianna's face was tense and flushed red. Jack could tell he'd crossed into the danger zone. Adrianna, daughter of a former marine, knew very well how to hold her own and wasn't one to back down when angered. Jack was just as stubborn when the moment warranted it. This was one such occasion.

She was worried about him, and he knew it. He had been battling his weight for the past six years. All indicators pointed to him being obese and likely to die of everything because of it. He glanced at himself in the reflective wall and sucked in his belly. *Not that bad, really.* No, he would fight the power and get the burger he wanted.

"I'm heading to Burger Zone. I'll see you in a few. If you are through first, can you find a table?" This was one of the moments that his manhood depended on him putting his foot down and winning the point. In a world of ever-increasing sissies, this was where one either joined the world of men-in-pretend or really stood out as a real man unwilling to take guff from his woman. He knew she'd back down eventually.

She rolled her eyes. "Fine. Enjoy hardening your arteries!" She stormed off, disappearing into the crowd. *I wonder how long I'll be doing damage control on that one. She left without getting her salad. She must be really pissed.* Jack sighed and walked to Burger Zone.

Jack imagined the man in front of him ordering, *I'd like a number 2, extra grease, and a helping of cholesterol please.* Jack stood watching the crowd while waiting for the man to complete his order. Sitting at a nearby table was a pretty brunette gently moving a stroller containing a small baby who was sleeping peacefully. It made him think of the day he and Adrianna had first brought their baby girl home from the hospital. It was such an exciting and scary time. Both he and Adrianna had very little exposure to babies so it was all very new and magical. Now he could change a baby's diaper while blindfolded.

Jack noticed the strange man he saw earlier in the parking lot. He appeared agitated and pacing back and forth near a garbage can. He was still muttering to himself and was rubbing his forehead. Tatters of his coat ran across the floor as he paced. He glanced continually at the woman and her baby. He pointed at the lady and turned away, grabbing his head.

"Can I help you?" the kid at the burger counter asked, obviously wishing she were somewhere else.

He stepped forward, trying to recall what he wanted to order, when the sounds coming from behind him suddenly changed. A chill crept up his spine. Something was not right. Jack turned his head to see why things felt the way they did. Out of the corner of his eye, he saw the crazy man with his jacket partly open. The brunette's face seemed to lose all color. Jack followed her gaze to the man's coat. Something about the outline under the coat appeared out of place. He focused on the tall man's hip section. A black clip jutted out — he had a gun!

Everything seemed to slow down. In one fluid motion, the tall man whipped aside his coat and pulled out an AK47. The back of his coat seemed to float behind him from the speed at which he moved. Screams erupted as the man fired a few bursts into the air. The next bursts released from the gun were not into the air, but into the crowd around him. The man, once just a creepy outcast in the crowd, now was a force of death. He didn't seem to have any reasoning for whom he targeted. He was simply firing at anything or anyone that moved. The once bustling food court was becoming a graveyard littered with the blood of the dead and dying.

The man paused and cackled, firing into the air. "The day of reckoning is coming. I am but a messenger. They are coming. Soon. All who stand against them will meet the fate they deserve." He fired at a man running for cover, and he fell to the ground, lifeless. "I don't want to do this, but you all need a lesson."

Unable to comprehend the fast change of events, Jack stood there motionless. *This can't be happening!* He watched helplessly as bodies overturned tables as they fell to the floor. Blood splattered against the walls. Screams of pain and fear echoed throughout the building.

POP! POP! POP! The janitor cleaning the lunch area took the bullets in his torso. He slumped forward, landing on his knees, pressing his hands to his chest. Blood seeped through his fingers. He shook violently as he slowly fell face-forward onto the floor.

Snap out of it! Get down, you idiot! But it was too late. The shooter saw Jack standing there – or maybe he didn't. Maybe he just happened to aim that way for the heck of it.

THUNK!

A bone-cracking sound radiated through Jack's brain, and a jolt of extreme pain sent him down to his knees, then to the floor. He rolled over onto his back. *Am I dead? No, not yet. Why did I have to insist on that damn burger? Goddammit!* The pain was coming from his left shoulder. He put his hand over it. It felt warm and sticky. *Fuck! My shoulder! He shot me!* He lay there and turned his head to the side. He saw the brunette still in her chair. Her head was tilted, blood dripping down her neck. She had taken one of the bullets in the head. The baby was still in the stroller, no longer fast asleep but shrieking out to its mother. *My God! How can anyone do this?*

POP! POP! POP!

The room was getting quieter – fewer people were screaming, yet the gunman still had rounds to go through and people to maim and murder. Jack imagined the baby as his own. He thought of Adrianna and Ashley, but thankfully they were not around. He hoped they would stay away from this carnage. Pain shooting through his side, he rolled onto his belly and used his good arm to prop himself up to get to his knees. The room seemed to fade in and out, his vision wavering. He looked up to see the baby still crying. A bullet ricocheted off the table two inches from the baby's stroller, showering it with broken bits of particle board and debris.

A large muscular man, now a short distance behind the shooter, seemed to be trying to sneak up on him. *That baby is going to be shot!* With that thought, he hoisted himself up to his feet and struggled to get to the baby's stroller. Just as he managed to release the baby from its safety straps, he and the shooter locked eyes. Jack saw nothing but emptiness. No emotion or reaction to the carnage around him. This man was pure evil. *So, this is how I go?* Jack smiled at the man who was pointing the gun at him and turned his back, protecting the baby in his arms.

POP! THUNK! POP! THUNK! POP! THUNK!

Jack fell to the floor with three bullets in his back. Landing on his side with the baby cradled in the crook of his arm, Jack gently rolled the baby to its back onto the floor. He could see the pool of blood escaping from his body, beneath his side. *God, I wish I could kiss my little girl one more time.* A tear rolled down the side of his face. The pain seemed to be fading — now there was more of a dull throbbing, much like a wound feels after the relief from a good painkiller.

Too weak to move, Jack looked into the baby's eyes, staring back at him. "You better be worth it kid," he said as his vision faded until complete darkness enveloped him.

—-End of Sample—-

Jack's story doesn't end here.

Step into the next chapter of the nightmare in *Conduit:
The Beginning*.

Scan the QR code or follow the link below to continue.

https://books2read.com/u/38O2Xd?format=all

Also by James Alexander

The Conduit Series

Conduit: The Beginning Link:

https://books2read.com/ap/8NojOj/James-Alexander

Conduit: The Surge Link:

https://books2read.com/b/mv9dRl

Conduit 3 (coming soon)

Psychological Thrillers

The Choice Link:

https://books2read.com/b/bWYgvq

Short Fiction (Sci Fi & Psychological)

Lost In Transit Link:

https://books2read.com/b/3yyBK6

Custodian of Justice Link:

https://books2read.com/b/3yMP9e

The Toothfairy Link:

https://books2read.com/b/boz2w1

Short Fiction (Humorous Dark Fantasy)

Statin's Revenge Link:

https://books2read.com/b/baxNGP

Collections & Bundles

Coming Soon

To View James Alexander's Full Portfolio scan the QR code:

https://writerjamesalexander.com

About the Author

James Alexander writes psychological and speculative fiction that explores the hidden edges of human consciousness, the mysteries of identity, and the forces-seen and unseen-that shape our world. Drawn to stories that blend tension, emotion, and the uncanny, he creates character driven narratives where the unknown is as internal as it is cosmic. A lifelong explorer of science fiction, technology, and the strange possibilities that lie just beyond ordinary life, James brings a grounded, human perspective to the extraordinary. When he's not writing, he enjoys diving into information technology, spending time with his kids, tinkering with home projects (with mixed results), and imagining new worlds and unsettling what-ifs. He is a lifelong resident of Maine, USA.

His fiction often delves into the darker frontiers of science—**colonization, genetic engineering, and first contact**—using these forces as pressure points that reveal who people become when the familiar world gives way to the unknown.

If you'd like to explore more of his work or follow along as new stories take shape, you can visit his website or join his newsletter for occasional updates, bonus fiction, and glimpses into the ideas that inspire his worlds.

https://www.subscribepage.com/jalexander_newsletter